An Amish Healing
& Ollie's Story

AN AMISH HEALING & OLLIE'S STORY

BETH WISEMAN

THORNDIKE PRESS
A part of Gale, a Cengage Company

Copyright © 2024 by Elizabeth Wiseman Mackey.
Thorndike Press, a part of Gale, a Cengage Company.

ALL RIGHTS RESERVED
This novel is a work of fiction. Names, characters, places, and incidents are either products of the author's imagination or used fictitiously. All characters are fictional, and any similarity to people living or dead is purely coincidental.
NO AI TRAINING: Without in any way limiting the author's (and publisher's) exclusive rights under copyright, any use of this publication to "train" generative artificial intelligence (AI) technologies to generate text is expressly prohibited. The author reserves all rights to license uses of this work for generative AI training and development of machine learning language models.
Thorndike Press® Large Print Christian Fiction.
The text of this Large Print edition is unabridged.
Other aspects of the book may vary from the original edition.
Set in 16 pt. Plantin.

**LIBRARY OF CONGRESS CIP DATA ON FILE.
CATALOGUING IN PUBLICATION FOR THIS BOOK
IS AVAILABLE FROM THE LIBRARY OF CONGRESS.**

ISBN-13: 978-1-4205-2067-5 (hardcover alk. paper)

Published in 2025 by arrangement with Beth Wiseman.

Print Number: 1   Print Year: 2025
Printed in Mexico

To Casey Roberts

TABLE OF CONTENTS

AN AMISH HEALING 9

OLLIE'S STORY 177

An Amish Healing

GLOSSARY

- **ach:** oh
- **boppli:** baby
- **daed:** dad
- **danki:** thank you
- **Englisch:** those who are not Amish; the English language
- **Gott:** God
- **gut:** good
- **haus:** house
- **kind/kinner:** child/children
- **lieb/liebed:** love, loved
- **mamm:** mom
- **mei:** my
- **mudder:** mother
- **nee:** no
- **Ordnung:** written and unwritten rules in an Amish district
- **rumschpringe:** running around time for teenagers, beginning at 16 years old
- **wie bischt:** hello/how are you?

- **wunderbaar:** wonderful
- **ya:** yes

CHAPTER 1

"There were no survivors." The sheriff spoke the words as if he were delivering a weather report, a man conditioned for this sort of thing.

Jeremiah could barely breathe as he stood on his parents' front porch shivering, his breath clouding in front of him as he fought to find any words, inhibited by the enormous knot in his throat.

To his left, his mother wept openly, and his father stood next to her with his hands stuffed in the pockets of a heavy black coat, his eyes focused on his black leather boots.

"*Danki* for coming to tell us personally," Jeremiah said when his parents seemed incapable of verbalizing their grief. His mother's sister, Nellie, her husband, John, and their driver had been killed in a fatal crash while traveling home to Montgomery, Indiana after spending two weeks visiting Jeremiah and his family in Pennsylvania. A seasoned driver for Amish families traveling from state to state, and familiar with ice on the roads, Charles Hoover had miscalculated his time to hit the brakes, sliding sideways and ultimately into a ravine where the car exploded into flames. They were only a few miles from home when the accident occurred.

Jeremiah and his parents knew that no one could have survived, but hearing the official report propelled their grief to a new level, especially for his mother who excused herself with a tearful nod of her head before she entered the farmhouse where Jeremiah had grown up.

"I'm sorry for your loss." The sheriff handed a business card to Jeremiah as his forehead crinkled. "I wrote my cell number on the back . . ." He tipped the rim of his sheriff's hat and scratched his forehead. The older man's eyebrows softened with a bit more sympathy than his delivery of the news only moments ago. "Uh . . . in case you need anything."

Jeremiah could only manage a nod before the sheriff turned to go down the porch steps, rushing to his patrol car with a hand to his forehead as he blocked the wintry mix of ice and snow that had been plummeting Paradise, Pennsylvania, for three days.

His father sighed, then shuffled into the house, gently closing the door behind him.

Jeremiah stood trembling on the porch, wishing he could go to his own home and unleash the emotions that were breaking his heart and crushing his spirit. *How could God let this happen?*

Nellie was ten years younger than his mother and her only sibling. His aunt was thirty-two, only ten years older than Jeremiah. She and John had been trying to have a baby for a decade, and they had recently been to an English doctor about possible fertility options, something that had been approved by the bishop.

Jeremiah folded his arms across his chest as he continued to tremble from a mixture of cold and despair. Logically, he knew in his mind that time would heal, but his heart felt otherwise, and it was hard not to feel bitterness toward God. Two relatives were stripped of a future, along with the driver who had always been a friend to many Amish families.

Jeremiah's people were taught that everything happens according to God's will, but right now, he didn't want to talk to the Lord. He needed to go inside and console his parents as best he could, but as he shifted his weight from one foot to the other, his hands deep in his pockets, he clinched his fists, looked up with his eyes closed as a tear fell, and said aloud, "Why, *Gott*?"

When he didn't hear an answer from God, or feel the healing presence he longed for, he slowly went into the house.

His mother sat on the couch with her face in her hands, bent at the waist, as his father stoked the fire, sending orange embers shimmying upward.

Jeremiah wanted to tread lightly. The initial news had invoked a reaction in his mother that he'd never witnessed, a painful wailing the day before that stabbed Jeremiah in the heart.

As he hung his heavy coat on the rack and slipped out of his black boots, he took a deep breath and made his way to the rocking chair in the corner. He closed his eyes and envisioned the room filled with family and friends only a few days ago. His mother had spent days in the kitchen cooking before his aunt and uncle's arrival, and visitors came and went for almost two weeks. Even with the steady snow and ice, folks had braved the weather, and a festive post-Christmas environment had left Jeremiah even more anxious to begin a family of his own. He'd spent two years remodeling an old farmhouse that had sat far too long following the death of Widow Mary Mae, the last living survivor in her family. He had created a perfect homestead with no one to share it with. He'd dated plenty, but the right woman hadn't come along.

His father still had his back to them when he said, "We will travel to Indiana as soon as possible when we know the arrangements." There was a long pause. "I will seek permission from the bishop for us to fly there. It's often allowed in situations such as this."

Jeremiah's adrenaline spiked, briefly sidestepping his grief. He'd never been in an airplane.

He shook the thoughts from his mind as guilt wrapped around him, and he refocused on the loss of his aunt and uncle. It was surreal to him that they no longer existed, at least not in their physical sense here on Earth. Jeremiah recalled the long visits he'd had with Nellie and John over the past ten years since they'd relocated to southern Indiana. He was only twelve when his parents put him on a bus to travel for the first time from Pennsylvania to Indiana. He'd made the trip twice a year, staying two to three weeks each time.

When he was young, his uncle took him

everywhere with him, proudly introducing him as his nephew. And John loved to throw a baseball back and forth, something Jeremiah's father wasn't fond of. Recollections swirled around in his mind, and maybe one day they would meld into beautiful memories. Right now, he felt as though he'd been knocked off balance, and he wondered if he would ever regain his footing.

He wouldn't ever be able to sneak out to the barn with his uncle to enjoy a few puffs of a cigar, something John allowed when Jeremiah had gotten older. It was a secret they shared even though Jeremiah suspected Nellie knew, choosing to turn a blind eye. He was close to his aunt, but the bond he shared with his uncle was the closest relationship he'd had outside of his parents.

As recollections of his time with Nellie and John ebbed and flowed into crashing waves of despair, he took a deep breath to keep control of his emotions.

But random memories plowed to the forefront of his thoughts. He would never have his aunt's award-winning blueberry cobbler or see the sweet smile that Nellie was known for.

Would his mother recover from this loss? Would Jeremiah?

He sat silently when his father continued

to move logs around in the fireplace and his mother started to cry harder, making it difficult for Jeremiah to hold back the tears pooling in the corners of his eyes.

"They should have never moved there," his mother said between her sobs. "This was their home." She dabbed at her eyes. "I would have visited more often if I'd known that . . ."

As her voice trailed off, Jeremiah lowered his head. Even though he'd continued his visits twice a year into adulthood, his mother hadn't made the trip nearly as often, citing the need to stay behind to take care of Jeremiah's father and her household duties.

But his mother had traveled to Indiana a year ago to visit his aunt and uncle. Jeremiah had stayed behind to help his father with an overload of construction projects he'd been contracted to do. Jeremiah had been bitter about not going, feeling cheated out of time with Nellie and John. But now he was glad that his mother had made the trip. And, despite the tragic circumstances, he was thankful that Nellie and John had recently visited.

Jeremiah recalled his uncle making the announcement ten years ago that he would be taking Nellie to a small town in southern

Indiana — Montgomery — where he was sure his construction company would flourish. And he'd been right. Lancaster County's population and touristy influx of visitors had made it more competitive for vendors in every type of occupation.

Nellie and John might have grown up in Lancaster County, but Indiana was their home now, and Jeremiah was sure preparations were in the works for their burial in three days, which was customary. First there would be a viewing in his aunt and uncle's home before everyone would travel to the cemetery for a final farewell.

Finally, his father joined his mother on the couch. "I will speak to the bishop about flying to Indiana." His father's voice was shaky as he spoke.

"Elijah, I do not want to stay at Nellie and John's *haus*." Lavina Huyard was normally a pillar of strength, and she had gotten through hard times in the past — deaths, cancer scares, and financial woes. But Jeremiah had never seen his mother consumed by so much grief. Maybe because Nellie was her only sibling. Maybe that wouldn't have mattered. The love of family might not be based on the number of members. Jeremiah was an only child, but not by choice. His parents had wanted a large family, but the Lord hadn't seen fit to bless them with more than Jeremiah. Maybe it was in their genes since his aunt and uncle had so much trouble trying to conceive, and sadly left this world without any children to be their legacy. Jeremiah hoped to someday fill his house with children, which would spill over into his parents' home, blessing them with lots of grandchildren even though he hadn't found the right woman to share his life with yet.

"Where will we stay?" Jeremiah finally asked.

"I will find us somewhere appropriate nearby." His father sat beside his mother on the couch, reached for her hand, and squeezed before pulling her close to him. It was a rare act of affection, and Jeremiah was pleased to see his father stepping into this nurturing role since it was his mother who always displayed compassion when others were hurting or in need of a hug.

After a few moments of silence, aside from the crackling of the fire and his mother's quiet whimpers, Jeremiah stood. "It stopped snowing. I should go."

He walked to his mother, leaned down, then kissed her on the forehead. "I *lieb* you, *Mamm*." They were weak words of comfort, but it's all he could say, fearful he would cry in front of her.

She nodded, which was enough for Jeremiah.

He was almost to the door when his father said, "I will let you know our travel plans, how we should handle the business, and other details tomorrow." His father didn't get off the couch or loosen his embrace with Jeremiah's mother.

"*Ya,* okay." Jeremiah put on his coat, then slipped into his boots.

He wasn't even to his buggy when warm tears rolled down his face, quickly feeling like an icy river as the wind swooshed and swayed.

For sure, he felt grief about his aunt and uncle, but he wasn't sure what was worse — his own feelings or seeing his mother in such despair.

CHAPTER 2

Ada Glick loaded a large basket with whoopie pies, snickerdoodle cookies, and kiffels — an old Pennsylvania Dutch recipe that had been passed down for generations in most Amish families. The English referred to the cookies as walnut horn cookies. In a separate box, she carefully placed a sugar cream pie. She'd prepared the baked goods yesterday when she heard that Esther — a co-owner of The Peony Inn — was down with her back and expecting guests at their bed and breakfast today. The visitors were traveling from Lancaster County, Pennsylvania, to attend the funerals for Nellie and John Troyer who had died tragically following a visit to see their family in Pennsylvania. The Troyers had been killed in a car crash, along with a driver from Pennsylvania.

She took a deep breath and said a quick prayer for all those who loved the Troyers. She also prayed for safe travel for the family coming to town.

Ada didn't know the Troyers well. They'd been in Montgomery for ten years, but Nellie was nine or ten years older than Ada, and even in their small community, they occupied different circles. Ada had attended quilting parties with Nellie Troyer, and she saw the couple every other Sunday at worship service. They'd always been friendly and kind to her. She would attend the funerals, along with most of the community.

After she slipped into her winter coat, she placed her black bonnet over her prayer covering, pulled on her boots, and prepared to brave the frigid temperature. Thankfully, the snow had stopped, and it had warmed up enough the day before to melt most of the ice on the roads. Ada cradled her basket with her elbow, picked up the box, and stepped outside. Her breath billowed in front of her as strands of strawberry-blonde hair escaped from beneath her prayer covering and bonnet.

She took her first step down from the porch but caught something out of the corner of her eye. After peering over her shoulder, she backed up a step until she was on the porch, eying the black, brown, and white furry critter shivering behind one of her rocking chairs. She placed her basket atop the box and put the baked goods in one of the four rocking chairs farthest from where the dog was sheltering.

"*Wie bischt, mei* little friend." She moved slowly, hoping she wouldn't spook the animal. There was blood on one of his front legs and a cut on his nose. She squatted down a couple feet away, expecting the dog might growl if she approached too quickly. Or bite.

Ada was the unofficial veterinarian in her small Amish community in Montgomery, Indiana. It was a title she'd earned by accident when a mother hen and her brood wandered onto her property following a long span of time without any rain in the area. All the chicks were malnourished, and the hen was in no shape to help them. Ada had been sure most, if not all, of the birds would die. Several folks who had visited her during that time agreed, some even saying she was wasting her time bottle feeding the little ones and even letting them inside the house when it got too hot outside. She'd built a pen in her mudroom.

Miraculously, all the birds survived, and when word got around, folks began to bring their injured or sick animals to Ada. She didn't mind. Ada loved all God's creatures, and while she didn't charge a fee, those who sought her services always left a little something in a jar she kept on the counter. When they asked how much, Ada would tell them, "Whatever you can afford." Folks had been generous, and with the sale of her baked goods, cookbooks, and other handmade items at the market, she was able to make a decent living for a woman on her own.

She inched closer to the injured dog. *"Wie bischt,"* she repeated barely above a whisper. "Are you going to let me help you?"

The animal continued to shiver, but he didn't show his teeth or growl. She reached out and offered the topside of her hand, and when the dog sniffed her hand and resituated his weight, she saw that it was a male, possibly a Border Collie pup. She also saw more blood underneath him.

Ada tried to keep her hands from shaking as she gingerly stroked the dog's back, drawing dirt and icy mud from its fur. She needed to get him inside and out of the cold. Depending on his injuries, he might nip at her, but she forged ahead and slipped both hands underneath the animal.

As she lifted him into her arms, he yelped but didn't snap at her. Instead, he lowered his head into the nook of her arm, his limp body still shivering as she made her way indoors and straight to the bathroom. She wrapped him in a towel, still cradling him in her arms as she retrieved her bag and box of goodies from the porch, placing them on the kitchen table. Her delivery would have to wait. This poor pup needed immediate attention.

Most Amish women had a sewing room. Ada had a make-shift veterinary office, complete with a metal exam table that the Lantz brothers had made for her. And she had just about every over-the-counter medication to treat most animal ailments. An English veterinarian had taught her how to stitch up an animal's wound and based on the amount of blood dripping from the animal and down her dark blue dress, she hoped she might be able to get this little fellow back to good health. But there had been plenty of times that internal injuries had prevented her from saving the lives of some animals. In those cases, she encouraged the owners of their pets to seek out a veterinarian in town.

She unwrapped the dog and laid a clean white towel on the cold metal table, then gently placed the dog on the surface. The billowy towel began to absorb dirt and blood, and Ada got to work, inspecting every inch of the animal. His panting was labored but unlike that of an animal about to take his last breath. His shivering had stilled. Her office was warm from the propane heater she'd clicked on when she entered the room, and the embers from an earlier fire in the living room continued to provide heat, spreading throughout her small home.

First, she needed to find out where most of the blood was coming from, and as she eased the dog onto his side, she identified what appeared to be his worst wound, a deep and dirty gash on the left side of his abdomen. "*Ach, mei* friend, we're going to need to stitch this up." She flinched. "I'm sorry."

She reached for a bottle of homemade herbs, mixed it with a little warm water in a shallow bowl, then offered it to the dog. She'd had the formula approved by the local vet in town, reluctantly. He always encouraged her to send folks his way, and rightly so since he was the one with a medical degree. But her people always sought her help first, and sometimes refused her recommendation to seek more qualified care. In those cases, Ada did the best she could. She'd lost a few, but she had saved a lot too.

The dog sniffed the bowl, then began to

lap up the watery formula with a vengeance until it was empty.

"There you go." Her concoction was filled with herbs that would help to calm the animal. Next, she reached for a bottle of salt water. "This will sting a bit." Ada had to get the wound clean before she could stitch it up. She didn't think it would require more than a few sutures, but when the salty water met with the dog's matted wound, he did nip at her. It was more of a warning, but his panting picked up again. Hopefully, the herbs would calm him soon.

She held a compress against the wound until most of the bleeding had stopped, then she rubbed a numbing solution all around the area and offered the dog more water filled with stronger herbs that would act as an anesthesia. She always offered a small amount in the beginning because some animals didn't tolerate it well.

It took her about an hour to stitch up the dog's deepest wound, then clean and bandage other areas so infection wouldn't set in. Luckily, she didn't have any furry overnight visitors, and when she was done, she carefully placed the dog in a kennel she kept in the room for overnight stays.

"You look like a new doggy," she said as she gently rubbed the side of the pup's face.

He had a bandage on his nose, one across his left ear, and another over the area she had just stitched. Overall, her new friend had tolerated her treatment well, growling slightly, but he hadn't nipped at her again.

Having gotten him all cleaned up, he looked more like a Border Collie mix, perhaps not full-blooded. He had dark hair on his back that was smooth now, unmatted from his journey. The top of his head was white, and a line of white ran down his nose and surrounded his mouth. His lower body was also white, clean now, after being drenched in mud.

She stood back and eyed the animal with his protective doggie collar around his neck. It was a soft blue blow-up collar so he could rest his head against it. She hated to leave the pup, but she didn't think she'd be gone more than an hour, hopefully less. The Peony Inn was only a ten-minute ride by buggy. She saw out the window that it wasn't snowing, and the sun was shining.

Ada sat on her stool and watched the dog until he fell asleep, fearing he would be terrified when he woke up in a kennel in a new place. But based on the mud that was caked to his wounds, he had traveled a good distance before he arrived on her front porch. Maybe the warmth and protection from the elements would give him comfort. As best she could tell, the animal didn't have any type of internal injuries, but once he was up and walking, she could get a better feel for his condition.

When he was well enough to travel by buggy, Ada would take him to her veterinarian friend to verify that Ada had done all she could, and she'd also have Dr. Farley check for a microchip. This fellow appeared to be less than a year old, and surely someone was missing him.

CHAPTER 3

Jeremiah's back ached as he came down the stairs of The Peony Inn. He'd carried his red suitcase upstairs, then both of his parents' suitcases, at his insistence. Jeremiah's heart ached, for sure, but his mother had sobbed through the entire funeral, and his father's bottom lip had trembled during the service. They were all exhausted, mentally and physically.

It wasn't the way of their people to show outward grief since the *Ordnung* taught them that death was a celebration of the life they'd lived. But no amount of teachings or rules could control how a person feels, and sometimes it was impossible not to outwardly show grief. Surely, God couldn't fault them for that, any more than Jeremiah should be faulting God for their deaths. *All things that happen are of His will,* he reminded himself, hoping to dissolve the bitterness he felt about the losses.

They had gone straight to Nellie and John's house upon arrival in Montgomery that morning before they'd even checked into The Peony Inn, barely making it in time for the viewing and funeral. The bishop had approved flying, as was often the case for out-of-state funerals. His father had paid top dollar to secure flights two days after they'd learned about Nellie and John's passing, causing them to take a late flight the night before. None of them had flown before, and although Jeremiah and his mother had slept through most of the flight, when he was awake, he saw his father white knuckling the armrests.

As was customary, members of the community had washed his aunt and uncle's bodies and prepared them for burial in unadorned, hand-built coffins before they had arrived. Being in his aunt and uncle's house for the funeral seemed to shake his mother even more as she cried through most of the service. It had the opposite effect on Jeremiah. Despite his sadness, he was able to breathe in the familiar scent of a home he'd spent a lot of time in, somehow infusing good memories into his mind at such a bad time. It was a current of sadness, loss, and memories, but in a strange way, it offered a small level of comfort.

After the Indiana bishop concluded the service, a caravan of buggies traveled single file to the Amish cemetery not far from his aunt and uncle's house.

The folks in Montgomery were kind to him and his parents at the service, and before he reached the bottom of the stairs at The Peony Inn, and despite his grief, he couldn't ignore the wonderful aromas wafting his way from the dining room, where he heard his father's voice. They'd eaten a huge meal at Nellie and John's house, another custom. But it was clear his mother didn't want to be there, around her sister's things in front of so many people. There hadn't been any discussion about what would happen to John and Nellie's house and belongings.

He meandered toward the smell of food, knowing he was expected to be polite and dignified. He would have rather stayed in his room upstairs and cried. It was still surreal — and unfair — that he wouldn't see Nellie and John again.

He eyed the enormous spread of food covering a dining room table that looked like it could hold twenty people. The chairs had been pushed against the wall, and some extra ones probably added, and there was a crowd of about twenty gathered in the large room. Several women encircled his mother in a protective and understanding stance. His father was speaking with two of the elders Jeremiah recognized from the funeral. Jeremiah was full from the meal earlier, but he didn't see himself resisting some of the offerings laid out.

He was eyeing the platters of food when his heart skipped an unexpected beat. A young Amish woman — perhaps around his age, early twenties — stood alone and gazing at a beautiful grandfather clock against the far wall. What set her apart were the strands of strawberry-blonde hair that had fallen loose from beneath her prayer covering. He could only see her from the side, but when she turned to face him, his heart did another flip in his chest.

She was tall and slender, wearing a dark, black dress like the other women. She had ivory skin and radiant hazel eyes. He wasn't sure he'd ever seen a lovelier woman in his life. Under different circumstances, he would have instantly wanted to know her. But he lived in Paradise, Pennsylvania. She most likely lived here in Montgomery, Indiana. Geography wasn't in their favor. And the timing was off. Besides, this woman was bound to have a husband. English men and women wore wedding rings as an outward token of their bond. Amish men grew a beard when they were married, and not before. Jeremiah had always wished there was a way to tell if an Amish woman was married, but there wasn't.

He looked down when a small person yanked on the sleeve of his black jacket.

"We haven't met," the small elderly woman said. "I'm Lizzie, one of the owners of The Peony Inn. I'm very sorry about what happened." She lowered her gaze. "Nellie and John were wonderful people and *liebed* by many here in our small community. They will be missed." She sniffled, dabbed her nose with a handkerchief, then lifted her eyes to his. "I'm told that you are Nellie and John's nephew." She shook her head. "Sometimes, it's hard to understand *Gott's* will for us when something so tragic happens."

Jeremiah nodded but couldn't help but stare past the tiny gray-haired woman. The beautiful strawberry-blonde woman was staring at him. He must have looked at her for too long because Lizzie spun around to see what — or who — he was looking at, then turned back to him with a smile that crooked up on one side.

"That's Ada Glick. Isn't she beautiful?"

Jeremiah nodded, fighting the urge to say

she was the loveliest woman he'd ever seen. "Is she married?" He felt his face turning red after he'd asked the inappropriate question. "I didn't mean — uh, I'm sorry . . . I . . ."

Lizzie had his arm again and was practically dragging him toward the woman who held his gaze.

"Ada, this is Jeremiah Huyard, Nellie and John's nephew." Lizzie grinned, which somehow didn't seem as inappropriate as Jeremiah asking if this lovely woman was married.

Ada clasped her hands in front of her and continued to lock eyes with him. "I am very sorry about this tragedy. Nellie and John were lovely people, and you have *mei* deepest sympathies."

He wondered how well Ada knew them. "I — I didn't see you at the funeral." Did he sound accusatory? He didn't mean to, but he would have noticed her.

"*Ya*, I was there," she said sweetly. "But I was mostly in the kitchen helping to prepare the food." She waved an arm across the fully loaded table. "Some of us also left early to bring what was left here, in case you and your parents were hungry later or would feel more comfortable without being in such a big crowd."

He nodded but didn't take his eyes from hers. "Very kind of you."

Lizzie cleared her throat. "Jeremiah asked if you were married." Jeremiah wished there was a trap door beneath him so that he could fall out of sight. His face was bound to be bright red. "So, I'll let you two chat." Lizzie spun on her heels, briskly walked away, and joined a large older man who held a plate with pie. She leaned up, whispered in his ear, then giggled.

Somewhere amid the awkward comments, Jeremiah had looked away, and now he was hesitant to look back at Ada.

"You can relax," she said as she gently laid a hand on his arm, sending a wonderful chill up his spine. He wished he didn't have on his dark suit coat or the crisp white shirt underneath so that he could feel her touch. "Lizzie — and her sister, Esther, who is upstairs and under the weather — are known matchmakers, and they snatch any opportunity to gently guide people into a relationship." She smiled. "Actually, that's not true. They try to *push* people together. Their intentions are always *gut,* but Lizzie's timing is sometimes . . . bad." Her smile slipped away, replaced by a sad frown. "I must apologize for Lizzie."

"*Nee,* that's not necessary," he said as he

forced a smile. He wished he could ask her if the sisters were ever successful with their matchmaking efforts. But he stopped himself from asking another unsuitable question.

"How long will you be staying here in Montgomery before you travel home to Pennsylvania?" Her hands remained clasped in front of her, her stance somewhat rigid, and her face flushed slightly.

He had an impulsive temptation to say *"forever."* But he shrugged. "I'm not sure. *Mei mamm . . .*" He glanced across the room at his mother, still encircled with a group of women. "*Mei mamm* isn't taking the loss well at all. Nellie was her only sibling." Jeremiah was glad he was able to speak without his voice shaking. He was tied up in knots of sadness, but this woman was making him come undone.

Ada flinched. "*Gott* be with her — and you and your *daed.* Grief is a process." For the first time, she avoided his eyes and drew in a deep breath before pursing her lips together, and she looked down. "It's always hard to understand *Gott's* will at a time like this."

Jeremiah sensed that she had felt the pang of grief. "*Ya,* it is." He glanced around the room again, no longer wanting to hide upstairs. "Would you like to step outside?" It was bold, but he didn't know how much time he had with this woman. His mother might decide to leave tomorrow morning.

She pointed toward the window, smiling slightly. "It's, um, . . . snowing."

Jeremiah followed her eyes to the glistening flurries drifting downward as if the clouds were melting and leaving delicate orange hues in the background, the sun barely peeking through. "Of course." He fought the rush of embarrassment rising from his neck to his face.

"It's been lovely to meet you, and I wish you and your family safe travels if I don't see you again before you leave." She held his gaze as she smiled. "I'm afraid I have to leave."

Jeremiah nodded, his chest tightening. Knowing his mother, she would want to head back to Pennsylvania as soon as possible and deal with the house and her sister's belongings at another time when her emotions weren't so fresh.

"Danki," he said softly, struggling to find a reason for her to stay, but she turned and walked away. He watched her telling folks goodbye, including the older woman, Lizzie, who glanced at Jeremiah before frowning.

It was silly, but he was tempted to employ

Lizzie's skills — pushy or not — to get to know the beautiful Ada. Jeremiah had dated plenty of women, but none of them had caused his heart to flip in his chest the way it did today. God's perfect timing felt off.

As guilt began to squeeze his heart, he once again reminded himself that having such thoughts on the day they'd buried Nellie and John was improper. But as Ada Glick walked briskly to her buggy, her black cape flowing in the snowy breeze, Jeremiah knew he had to see her again.

CHAPTER 4

Ada pushed her horse as much as she could in the snowy conditions, anxious to check on her furry patient. But commingled with her concern for the rescued dog were images of Jeremiah Huyard floating around in her mind. As much as she would like to know him better — and he seemed to feel the same way — the timing wasn't good, he lived in another state, and she was needed at home.

She recalled the way his face had turned red when he'd asked her if she wanted to step outside which brought forth a smile. He was tall, muscular, and with a deep voice that made him sound older than he probably was. She guessed he was in his early twenties and clearly not married based on his clean-shaven face. Perhaps, under different circumstances . . . but it was likely she would never see the man again.

After tethering her horse, she tucked her

chin, pulled down the rim of her black bonnet, and trekked through the snow to her house. She heard loud whimpering before she was even to the front door.

She didn't drop her snow-covered shoes, cape, or bonnet by the door as she ran into the mudroom, leaving a snowy trail of white in her wake. Her patient was lying in a slightly different position as when she left, but when he heard her voice, he quieted.

"You poor *boppli.*" She unlatched the lever on the kennel and slowly reached a hand inside, gently stroking his back, one of the few places that didn't have a bandage. "I'm sorry I left you."

The animal struggled to stand, his legs shaky, but he made his way to her, then licked her on the nose.

"*Ya,* I'm back. Will you let me hold you?" She patted the entrance of the kennel, and the animal shuffled slowly toward her, then she carefully scooped him into her arms, cradling him like a baby to avoid the bandages on his nose, underbelly, and paw.

"You're shivering." She carefully laid him down on the couch, then hung her cape and hat on the rack by the front door as she wiggled out of her boots.

Ada added a log to the glowing embers in her fireplace, then sat on the couch and eased the animal into her arms. "Where did you come from?"

She lowered her face to his, almost touching the bandage on his nose, and he gave her a big wet kiss. He was still showing no indication of any internal injuries based on the way he moved his body. Ada would give him a few days to rest and heal, unless any other problems surfaced, then she would take him to Dr. Farley to check for a chip. More snow was forecast for the next couple of days anyway. She didn't want to take out the injured dog in such bad weather. She could hire a driver, but, in truth, she liked this new furry friend. And, somehow, this little fellow had landed on the doorstep of the resident veterinarian.

It wasn't long before the dog fell asleep in her arms, lightly snoring. Ada leaned her head against the back of the couch, closed her eyes, and thought about Jeremiah again. She'd never met anyone she'd felt instantly drawn to. She'd dated the few eligible bachelors in her small community, but none had given her the same tingly feeling as the stranger at the inn.

"Do you think I'll ever see that man again?" she asked the sleeping dog, who took up most of her lap and the nook of her elbow. "I'm thinking I won't."

Her thoughts drifted back to the dog and who might own him. How long had he been roaming? Would he have a chip so that his owners could be identified? Selfishly, Ada hoped he didn't. She'd helped a lot of pets, but she'd only had one dog of her own, and he had died from a rare blood disorder at an early age, which had broken her heart. But maybe it was time for her to have a pet, another warm body to ease the loneliness she felt sometimes.

She could hear her mother's words in her mind. "Ada, you need to move to Shipshewana with us where there are more opportunities for you."

Her parents had sold Ada's childhood home and made the move only a year earlier, but Ada loved Montgomery, the peace and quiet, and the knowingness that people sought her out to care for their beloved pets. Besides, she'd already put a down payment on her small farmhouse when her parents decided to make the move. She had been saving her money from babysitting since she was old enough to do so, and she'd continued to put away money she'd made from sales of her crafts. Even though she'd hoped to marry someday, there hadn't been any serious prospects, and she'd fallen in love with the house she now owned.

"If no one claims you, would you like to stay here?" She leaned down and touched her nose to the dog's snout, careful of the bandage. Then she chuckled. She could have sworn the dog nodded. "Then it's settled. And we need a name for you."

Ada startled when her phone rang in her small black purse. She'd forgotten to turn it off. The bishop allowed cell phones for some folks in her community, and Ada had been granted permission a year ago because of her care of animals. However, the features of the phone still felt foreign to her at times. She reached across the dog, who shifted slightly, and took the phone from her purse.

"*Wie bischt,* Lizzie," she said when she saw Lizzie's number on the screen. "Is everything okay?"

"I saw the way you and Jeremiah Huyard looked at each other today. He and his parents are leaving first thing in the morning. What are we going to do about that?" Lizzie huffed, never one to waste time on pleasantries, always straight to the point.

Ada resisted the urge to laugh because Lizzie would only scold her. "I don't think there is anything we can do about it."

"Ah ha!" Lizzie bellowed into the phone.

"You didn't deny the fact that there was something between the two of you!"

"Lizzie . . . the man is grieving, and he lives in another state. I think your matchmaking skills might be put to better use somewhere else." Ada felt a mixture of regret and sympathy . . . and guilt for thinking about Jeremiah, a man she didn't know, in a romantic way.

"They flew here so they would arrive in time for the funeral. But since they hired a driver to take them home, they won't be leaving before daybreak. I convinced them not to, told them they need a hearty breakfast before their driver begins the long drive back to Pennsylvania. If you get here by six in the morning —"

"*Nee*, Lizzie." Ada sighed. Even though she was always up by 4 a.m., which was customary for the Amish, she needed to be mindful of weather conditions for going out alone. "We have more snow on the way."

There was a long silence before Lizzie cleared her throat. "I'm really not feeling very well and could use some help tomorrow morning." The older woman coughed, and Ada stifled a smile since it didn't sound like a real cough.

"Now, Lizzie . . . would you really want me to travel alone in unsafe weather?" She was pretty sure her furry friend would be okay for a while on his own, and a part of Ada wanted nothing more than to bundle up tomorrow morning for a chance to see Jeremiah . . . but why? Would they exchange letters or become friends? Then she had a thought. "I'm sure the family will return to settle Nellie and John's affairs. If it's in *Gott's* plan for me to see Jeremiah again, then it will happen."

"*Nee,* they aren't coming back." Lizzie huffed again. "Earlier we had tea in the den, and the *mudder* — Lavina — said that they had spoken to a real estate agent about selling Nellie and John's *haus,* with instructions to sell the furniture with the *haus,* and to ship certain personal items to Lavina and Elijah, the father. Lavina said she couldn't bear to go through her sister's personal belongings just yet."

Ada's heart sank a little. In the back of her mind, she had considered that there might be a connection with Jeremiah and his family via the estate. "That's understandable."

"And you're right about the weather," Lizzie said, sounding defeated. "I don't want you putting yourself at risk. But it's just such a shame to see a connection like that and not be able to follow up on it."

"All things according to *Gott's* plan, *ya*?" Ada closed her eyes and revisited the memory of the way Jeremiah had gazed at her. But there had been three tragic deaths. She shook the thoughts from her mind.

"*Ya*, I guess."

"How is Esther? Is her back better?" Ada did feel badly that Lizzie didn't have any help for in the morning. Up until two weeks ago, they'd had a young woman staying at the inn and working for them. But, as with those before her, she'd left The Peony Inn to get married, after a successful matchmaking scenario run by Lizzie and Esther. Ada wondered if the two women realized that they kept matching up their help, leaving them to tend to the inn on their own.

"Esther is being Esther, doing things she shouldn't. She's supposed to stay in bed." She sighed. "It's okay. Ben is helping me while we try to keep Esther from overdoing it."

Lizzie's husband wasn't in the best of shape, but at least they were all there for each other in case of an emergency. If Ada really thought Lizzie needed help for breakfast tomorrow morning, she would brave the snow and go. But Lizzie had seemed just fine at the funeral and afterward, only a few hours earlier. And she hadn't coughed again throughout their conversation.

"I know Esther is hard to keep down." Lizzie's older sister was the exact opposite of Lizzie in many ways. She was a large woman, very dignified and soft-spoken. "I hope she will be fully recovered soon."

"Me too," Lizzie spoke softly. She and her sister might be opposites, but anyone who was around them could see how much they loved each other.

Silence.

"Lizzie, are you okay?" Ada took a deep breath. Maybe Lizzie really did need her help in the morning, or was that Ada's way to justify a trip in the snow to see Jeremiah? Things could get treacherous between her house and the inn if too much snow fell overnight.

"Ya, ya," Lizzie said softly. "I was just thinking about Nellie and John. They were *gut* people, and it's just so tragic the way they died. And, *ya,* I know we are supposed to accept these types of things as *Gott's* will and celebrate the lives they led. But . . . the way the car exploded, the awful —"

"I know. Tragic." Ada cut her off. It was too horrible to imagine.

More silence. Lizzie usually ended conversations abruptly when she didn't have anything else to say, so Ada waited.

"I feel like maybe we should have said something at the funeral, whether it was appropriate or not, about the young dog that perished along with them. They'd only had that Border Collie a few months, but Nellie and John adored him."

Ada froze as she glanced down at the pup in her lap. "I didn't know Nellie and John had a dog."

"They mostly kept him inside. A cute fellow with fluffy dark hair and a white nose." She chuckled. "He jumped in *mei* lap and licked *mei* nose every time I went to visit. I wasn't surprised when Lavina told me that Nellie and John had taken him on their trip to Pennsylvania. I think Lavina had gotten rather attached to the dog. I know it's not like a person, but folks get close to their pets."

Ada's chest tightened. "Um . . . did you say the dog was a Border Collie?"

"*Ya,* cute fellow," Lizzie grunted. "Well, I better go."

Lizzie hung up abruptly before Ada could say anything. She held her furry patient a little closer as she considered what Lizzie had said. Should she battle the elements in the morning and take the dog to The Peony Inn to see if it could possibly be Nellie and John's dog?

She shook the thought away. She'd seen the picture in the newspaper of the aftermath of the fire and the burned vehicle even though she wished she hadn't laid eyes on it. There was no way any person or animal could have survived the impact in the ravine or the flames that immediately followed.

Nee. This was not Nellie and John's dog, only a coincidence that her rescued animal resembled their deceased pet.

She stared at the bundle of fur in her lap, his eyes wide and searching hers. Then she picked him up and carried him to her bedroom. After she'd pulled back the covers, she laid him down on the pillow next to hers. She'd need to take him out to do his business before she fell asleep, but for now . . . she just crawled under the covers, reached over, and rubbed the dog's back until he closed his eyes, a gentle snore following.

Ada didn't need to get close to this dog in case Dr. Farley found a chip. Then she'd have to return the animal to its owners. But there was no way this could be Nellie and John's pet. That would be nothing short of a miracle.

CHAPTER 5

A week later, the snow had melted, and the sun beamed down on glistening dew. Her patient — whom she'd named Ollie — was well enough to bounce around in the yard and chase a tennis ball Ada had bought at the market. Only a small bandage remained on his nose, and she'd taken his stitches out that morning.

As she sat in one of the rocking chairs on her porch with a blanket wrapped around her, she considered waiting a few more days to take Ollie to the veterinarian. But that wasn't fair to whoever might own the dog. She was amazed at how attached a person could get to an animal in only a week. Sighing, she called for him. "Come on, Ollie, we need to get ready to go on a short trip." She puckered her lips and followed up with a weak whistle, but the dog got the point and ran up the porch steps, then licked her face when she squatted down.

"We better get ready to go see Dr. Farley. You might have an owner who is missing you." She scratched behind Ollie's ears as her chest tightened. It was wrong to pray that this dog didn't have a family to return to, but she asked God to let her keep the dog anyway.

She'd bathed him the night before, and despite his muddy paws, he was reasonably clean as she attached a leash, and they made their way to her buggy. She placed him in a travel-sized kennel, which was a tight fit, but he would travel safely that way.

Twenty minutes later, they arrived at Dr. Farley's office. When Ada had called yesterday, the receptionist told her they had an opening at ten this morning. When they walked into the small building, Ada looked at the clock on the wall. They were right on time. Her chest constricted again, the way it had done all morning. Soon, she would find out if Ollie had a family, and facing that possibility should have made her happy, but it didn't.

After ten minutes had passed, a young woman in blue scrubs with curly blonde hair welcomed her, then motioned her behind the door that led to the examination room.

"Dr. Farley will be right in," the woman

said before she closed the door.

Ada sat on the chair against the wall, and Ollie squatted at her feet, panting slightly.

"You're okay, Ollie." She scratched the top of his head, again wondering if she would be giving him up soon.

When Dr. Farley walked in, Ada stood and tried to smile at the white-headed man who towered over her.

He leaned his tall, stout body down and lifted the dog into his arms, placing him on a metal examination table. "Gloria said we're checking for a microchip today. I don't recognize this animal. If he has a chip, someone else must have inserted it."

"*Ya.*" She cleared her throat. "He's a stray that I've had for a week. The weather wasn't *gut,* and he needed stitches. Today is the first day I felt like he was fit for travel." A lie. She could have brought him two days ago. She'd ask forgiveness for her fib later. "Can you please check him out thoroughly and make sure I didn't miss anything and that the place where he had stitches looks okay?"

Dr. Farley inspected the dog, beginning with his previously sutured area, and onto his other spots where fur was just starting to grow back. Then he removed the bandage on his nose. "Ada, you've done good work."

He stretched the dog's mouth and shone a light inside. "This is only a guess, but he is probably ten or eleven months old, less than a year."

"I didn't think he was very old. He's playful and looks like he hasn't grown into his big paws yet." She hoped the growing knot in her throat didn't constrict her speech or that the tears welling in the corners of her eyes didn't spill.

Dr. Farley kept a hand on Ollie, but said, "Oh, dear. It looks like someone has gotten attached."

Ada swiped at her eyes. "*Ya,* I guess I have. But if he has owners who are missing him, then he should be returned."

"You have a good heart," Dr. Farley said as he smiled with sympathy. "Well, let's have a look. He took a step backward and picked up a round instrument, then started to scan around Ollie's neck, his back, and even down his legs . . . and relief began to rush over Ada.

Then there was a beep.

Ada drew in a deep breath before Dr. Farley briefly glanced her way, nodded, then reached behind him for a pen as he adjusted his gold-rimmed glasses and peered at the scanner.

Ada slowly let out the breath she was

holding, willing herself to be happy that the dog had an owner even if the emotion wasn't genuine. "I guess he belongs to someone."

Dr. Farley pushed his glasses on top of his head, picked up Ollie, and placed him in Ada's lap. "I know you're disappointed, Ada, but you did a fine job nursing this boy back to health, and I'm sure the owners will be grateful."

Not if it's Nellie and John's dog. Ada remained sure that couldn't be possible. It was unlikely that the animal even had Amish owners since most of their people didn't take their animals to veterinarians or have chips inserted. They just visited Ada instead.

"I need Gloria to run this registration number," Dr. Farley said. "I'll be back in a few minutes with the information." He smiled sympathetically at Ada again.

After the door to the small examination room closed, she pulled Ollie closer, leaned down, and rubbed noses with him. As a tear rolled down her cheek, her furry friend licked it away, then tipped his head to one side and locked eyes with her. He seemed to feel her sadness.

"You'll be going home to your owners soon," she said before swiping at her eyes. Hopefully, they would be kind people who would allow her to visit Ollie . . . Ollie, a name I gave him. "I wonder what your real name is," she said barely above a whisper as Ollie ran his tongue across her face again, the same way he did each morning when he felt it was time for her to wake up. He'd been sleeping in her bed all week.

She shook her head as she scratched him behind the ears. It was much too soon to have gotten this attached to a dog. And she would keep telling herself that even as she pictured handing the animal over to his rightful owners.

Dr. Farley walked into the room, his face ashen, his jowls drooping, as he locked eyes with Ada. "This animal is registered to Nellie and John Troyer." He scratched his cheek as he shook his head. "I saw the accident in the local newspaper. Such a terrible thing to happen, especially so close to home." Sighing, he leaned against the counter and stuffed his hands in the pockets of his crisp white doctor's coat. "I remember reading that they didn't have any family who lived nearby." He paused as his lips curled up slightly. "I guess Ollie is yours."

Ada wanted to be happy about this news, but was a dog like a child? Should the next of kin be notified? She bit her lip, telling herself to just nod and be quiet, but the truth erupted inside of her. "I met Nellie and John's family while they were here for the funeral." She glanced at sweet Ollie. "Nellie and John had taken Ollie — or whatever his real name is — with them to visit family in Pennsylvania. He was in the car during their commute home when the car exploded in the ravine." She squeezed the dog closer to her, wrapping her arms protectively around him. "He couldn't have survived." She searched Dr. Farley's face. "This can't be the same dog."

The kind veterinarian she'd known for the past few years sighed. "I had Gloria run the information twice on the scanner just to be sure. Maybe he was ejected out of the car before it . . . um, exploded."

Ada thought back to the burns on Ollie. At the time, they appeared to be road rash. "The right thing to do is . . ." She pressed her lips together, hesitant to verbalize the thought. "I should contact the family. Maybe they won't want him."

"Do you have a way to reach them?" He paused. "The law is that you are my client, and I would need your consent to share information with the registered owners. Technically, the decision is yours, whether to contact them."

Ada nodded, considering her options,

ultimately deciding that Jeremiah and his family wouldn't want the dog. "They stayed at The Peony Inn. I'm sure Lizzie and Esther have contact information." She recalled how many times she'd dreamed about seeing Jeremiah Troyer, but not under these circumstances.

She stood with Ollie in her arms. "*Danki*, Dr. Farley."

The older man nodded, then motioned for her to go ahead of him and out the door. He walked to the receptionist — Gloria — and handed her a piece of paper before he turned to Ada. "I have another patient, but I'm sure whatever decision you make will be the right one."

"I'll pray about it," she said as she blinked back tears and shuffled toward where Gloria was sitting behind a desk filled with paperwork and jars of dog treats.

"What do I owe you?" Ada asked as she placed Ollie on the cold gray floor, clasping his leash with shaky hands.

"No charge today, Miss Glick." The woman smiled.

Dr. Farley had never charged Ada for a visit, but she always asked.

She walked slowly to her buggy, secured Ollie in his kennel, then untethered her horse and climbed inside. She sat there, the sunshine warming the chill she felt on the outside. Inside, her stomach churned as she finally grabbed the reins and got the buggy on the main road.

There was one person who would know for sure if this was Nellie and John's dog. She was also the same person who had contact information for Jeremiah's family. She recalled Lizzie saying how Lavina had become attached to the dog. Perhaps having the animal to keep would give her some sort of comfort during this devastating period in her life. Seeking out Lavina and giving her that option was the right thing to do.

But when Ada got to the fork at the end of the two-laned highway, she stopped. Left was The Peony Inn. Right was the way to Ada's house.

She looked to her left, then to her right, before she sighed and made her decision.

CHAPTER 6

"You're doing the right thing," Esther said to Ada as she sat across the kitchen table from Lizzie, her husband, Benjamin, and Esther at The Peony Inn.

Ada had been almost home, ready to keep Ollie forever, but in her heart, she knew a woman in Pennsylvania might find comfort in knowing Ollie had survived. She planned to keep referring to him as Ollie until she learned his real name. Dr. Farley hadn't mentioned a name attached to the number he had scanned. If there was one, maybe he was doing her a kindness by not mentioning it. To Ada, he was Ollie.

She took a sip of coffee, her hands trembling as she fought back tears.

"*Ach,* hon." Lizzie reached across the table and laid a hand on Ada's. "I can see how hard this is for you." She glanced at Ollie in Ada's lap. "But that is definitely Nellie and John's dog. Although, I can't remember his name." She paused as if to let the news soak in for Ada. "I remember Nellie telling me that they had one of those chips placed in him because he couldn't wear a collar. He'd been stung by a bee and swelled up so badly that they had to take his collar off. They were worried he would choke to death if they weren't around and he got stung again, so that's when they decided to have the veterinarian implant the chip." She gave Ada's hand a slight squeeze. "Do you want me to make the call?"

Ada nodded. She didn't think she could get through a conversation with any of the family members without full-on sobbing. But as her pulse sped like a rushing river through her veins, she considered the possibility that keeping Ollie might be difficult for Lavina, a constant reminder of her lost loved ones. Maybe if she knew that Ollie was in a good home, she would decide to let Ada keep the animal.

Lizzie left the kitchen and returned less than a minute later with a mobile phone and a piece of paper. She scanned the notes on the slip of paper, then dialed a number, put the phone on speaker, and placed it in the middle of the kitchen table.

Ada recognized Jeremiah's deep voice

when he answered.

"This is Lizzie from The Peony Inn in Montgomery, Indiana." Lizzie glanced at Ada, then back at the phone. "Who am I speaking with, please?"

"*Wie bischt,* Lizzie. This is Jeremiah Huyard." He paused. "Did we leave something at your inn by mistake?"

"*Nee* . . . not really." Lizzie cleared her throat. "But I do have news for you. Um . . ." Even Lizzie was struggling to get the words out. "I know this might be hard to believe, but apparently John and Nellie's dog . . ." She looked at the animal in Ada's lap. "Uh . . . somehow their dog survived. I know it is . . ." Lizzie blinked her eyes a few times, and Ada wished she had made the call. It had nothing to do with Jeremiah. Lizzie had been closer to Nellie and John than she was, and her emotions were showing. "Or, um . . . was . . . their dog because I've seen the Border Collie at their *haus.* I can't recall his name." When there was an unusually long silence, Lizzie asked, "Are you still there?"

"*Ya.*" Jeremiah cleared his throat. "How can that be? I mean, the way *mei* aunt and uncle died . . ."

"It's a shock to all of us, Mr. Huyard. This is Esther, the other owner of The Peony

Inn." Esther had jumped in when Lizzie's voice became shaky. "The little fellow wandered onto the porch of our non-official veterinarian, and she nursed him back to health, then followed up with a vet in town where she learned he had a chip."

"That's unbelievable," Jeremiah said, followed by a long sigh.

Lizzie sniffled. "A miracle, really." Lizzie's eyes drifted to the dog in Ada's lap, then she locked eyes with Ada, the hint of a smile on her face. "You met the young lady who cared for the animal, Ada Glick, a lovely woman with strawberry-blonde hair. I believe I introduced you to her."

Ada could feel her cheeks flush. Lizzie obviously recognized this as an opportunity to play matchmaker, despite the circumstances. Ada would be lying to herself if she didn't admit that it was nice to hear Jeremiah's voice.

"Uh, *ya* . . . I do remember her."

"Mr. Huyard, we have you on speaker phone," Ada said. "I have your aunt and uncle's dog in *mei* lap, and your *mudder* told Lizzie and Esther how she had grown fond of the dog. We didn't know if having him would give the family comfort during this difficult time. But I want you to also know that I am happy to keep this little fellow if that isn't the case." She bit her bottom lip, hoping the latter would be true.

"*Nee, nee . . . danki* to you for calling. I feel sure *mei mamm* will want him. His name is Hank, by the way."

Ada couldn't help but cringe. Hank? She tried to disguise her disapproval by curling her lips up. He looked like Ollie to her. Then she cuddled the dog closer, fighting the growing knot in her throat. *I'm going to have to give him up.* She couldn't say anything.

"*Mei mamm* asked me if I would be willing to travel back to Montgomery to do some repairs on Aunt Nellie and Uncle John's *haus*. The realtor suggested the repairs. And I have instructions to gather up a few things that didn't make it home in the boxes we had shipped. So, I was planning to head that way in a couple of months. But I can move up *mei* trip to get the dog."

"There's no rush," Ada was quick to say. "He's fine staying with me until your arrival." Although Ada would be even more attached to the animal in a couple of months. She had fallen in love with him after only a week.

"*Nee*, it was already planned for me to travel there. I can just rearrange *mei* schedule to get there sooner." He paused. "Ada, I must thank you for tending to Hank. I know that Nellie and John would be grateful. They hadn't had the animal for long, but he is a sweet fellow."

Yes, he is. Ada pressed her trembling lips together but couldn't manage a response.

"Then, it's settled," Lizzie said. "You can correspond directly with Ada regarding your arrival date and time. Her phone number is . . ."

Ada's jaw dropped. Did Lizzie know everyone's phone number by heart or just hers?

But not even the thought of seeing Jeremiah again could brighten her mood. She was going to have to give up Ollie. And she wouldn't be able to visit the dog since he would be going back to Pennsylvania with Jeremiah.

Jeremiah thanked them all again, then pressed END on his phone. He had no idea if his mother wanted the dog or not. The pup might just serve as a reminder of all she'd lost. And even though retrieval of some family heirlooms and repairs to the home had been roughly scheduled for two months from now, next week sounded much better. He'd thought about Ada ever since he'd left Montgomery, looking forward to possibly seeing her in a couple of months. Now, there was a more urgent need for him to leave next week . . . or sooner.

He rubbed his chin from where he sat on his parents' couch. His folks were upstairs when their mobile phone rang. When Jeremiah saw it was a number from Indiana, he'd answered it, not thinking for a minute that it might be about Hank. How could the dog have survived?

Jeremiah was still pondering when his parents came down the stairs. The swelling underneath his mother's eyes had receded some, but she still looked tired, and he suspected she had a lot of sleepless nights and would for a long time.

"You're not going to believe this," he said, still rubbing his chin as he leaned back against the tan couch, crossing one ankle over his knee.

"What?" his father asked, frowning.

His father was a pessimist, forever expecting bad news. He'd always been that way, but more so lately. Business hadn't been good, and then Nellie and John's deaths had put some things behind schedule.

"While you were upstairs, a woman from The Peony Inn called." He stopped, unable to keep from smiling as he shook his head. "Hank survived the accident."

His mother had been on her way to the kitchen when she spun around and pressed her palms to her chest. "What?"

"*Ya*, that pup must have been ejected from the car and somehow made his way to the woman who is considered the resident vet for their district." He shrugged, still smiling a little. "She doctored him, and they want to know if you want him."

His mother smiled for the first time since before the funeral. She even bounced up on her toes. "*Ya, ya* . . . I would *lieb* to have Hank." His mother tapped a finger to her chin. "Someone pointed out the young woman with the strawberry-blonde hair while we were at The Peony Inn and said she took care of the animals at the inn. I think I saw you talking with her. Is that the person who has Hank?"

"*Ya,* it is."

Jeremiah's father sighed before he sat down in his recliner and picked up The Budget. His dad never missed reading the weekly edition of the newspaper that kept Amish and Mennonite communities in touch with each other throughout America. "We already have a dog," he grumbled, mostly under his breath. Jeremiah was sure his father wouldn't deny his mother anything right now, though.

Jeremiah could still see Ada's face in his mind's eye, her strands of light red hair brushing against her ivory skin. "But we can't wait two months before I go to Montgomery." He shrugged. "It's not fair to leave the dog with her that long." Even though Ada had said there was no rush, Jeremiah was anxious to see her again.

His father grumbled again, but Jeremiah didn't catch what he said. He'd already been upset that Jeremiah would have to spend time in Indiana to get Nellie and John's house ready to sell and gather the things his mother wanted. Jeremiah did most of the heavy lifting related to their construction company and would be missed.

His father sighed. "Go get the dog," he said before turning to his wife, smiling a little, and Jeremiah knew his father was happy to see his mother excited about something. "But try to wrap things up there and be back in a couple of weeks."

The real estate agent had called and made suggestions for repairs on the house, and a few things had been obvious the short time they were there. Some boards on the porch were loose, and there were places on the ceiling on the south side of the home that needed sheetrock repair, possibly from a water leak. They could sell it 'as is,' but he and his father agreed that it would sell for considerably more if it was in tip-top shape. And it was decided that it would be cheaper for Jeremiah to do the work and convenient since he could bring back the things his mother wanted.

He looked at the top of his left hand where he had quickly scribbled Ada's phone number when Lizzie had offered it.

After he stood from the couch and said he was heading home, he went to his mother and hugged her. "I'm glad this brings you a tiny bit of joy."

She squeezed him. "Nellie *liebed* that dog so much. I'm glad he survived. It will be like having a small part of her with me."

"I'm glad too," he said, meaning it. But he'd also get to see Ada much sooner than he'd thought.

He'd call her when he got home.

It had taken everything Ada had not to completely lose her composure in front of Lizzie, Benjamin, and Esther.

As she curled up in bed with Ollie, much too early for sleep, she had to admit she was anxious to see Jeremiah, but she would continue to hope that his mother wouldn't want her new furry friend.

71

When her phone buzzed on the nightstand, she took a deep breath and slowly answered. *"Wie bischt."*

"Wie bischt. Is this Ada?"

She recognized the deep voice on the other end of the line and gulped. "*Ya,* it is."

"This is Jeremiah." Hearing from him sent a quick jolt of electricity through her, a reminder of their initial meeting that stayed with her.

"First, I want to thank you for taking care of Hank. *Mei mamm* was thrilled to hear that he survived the accident, and she said it would be like having a small part of Nellie with her."

Ada squeezed her eyes shut and instinctively pulled Ollie closer to her. "So . . . that means she wants to keep him?"

"*Ya,* she does. I'll be heading your way in a few days. If you don't mind telling me your address, I can stop by on *mei* way to Nellie and John's *haus* and pick up Hank."

Ada cringed at the name again and rejoiced at the chance to see Jeremiah again. "*Ya,* all right." She cleared her throat, pushed back the knot growing there, then gave him her address before they said their goodbyes. She had wanted to stay on the call, but untangling her emotions would have made a longer conversation even more difficult.

She pulled Ollie into her lap, and he covered her in wet kisses. A double-edged sword for sure. Jeremiah had caught her attention right away when she'd met him, and she'd longed to see him again. But now she would lose Ollie.

Such silliness to allow myself to become so attached to this dog, she thought as she nuzzled his nose and fought tears. But she reminded herself that if Ollie brought half as much joy to a grieving woman as he had to her, then letting him go was the right thing to do.

She wouldn't make the same mistake with Jeremiah. For however long he was here, she'd keep her distance and not take a chance on getting close to him also.

CHAPTER 7

It ended up being three weeks later when Jeremiah arrived. His father had insisted that he help him finish a big decking project surrounding an English friend's house. His mother had been concerned about leaving the dog with Ada for so long, arguing for Jeremiah to go to Indiana sooner. In the end, his father had the final say.

Jeremiah had communicated his travel arrangements with Ada, even trying to infuse a little small talk, but she was stoic and seemingly not interested in much he had to say, which was disappointing. Maybe she would be different in person.

He traveled by taxicab from the Indianapolis Airport to Ada's house, which took him through several cities before arriving in the rural town of Montgomery. After paying the driver, he walked slowly up the path that led to her house toting a red suitcase his mother had given him to use. He would have preferred a knapsack or backpack, but in the end, his mother had been right to insist on a larger piece of luggage. Spring was on the horizon, but he suspected evenings in Indiana were still chilly enough for a coat.

Ada's farmhouse wasn't very big, but the yard was pristine for this time of year. As the signs of winter lingered, there were tiny sprouts of growth peeking out of flowerbeds that had been weeded and cleared. Enormous and abundant Ash trees reached toward the clouds. Several bird feeders were attached to tree branches, and cardinals and blue jays were plentiful, fluttering away as he passed. Ada's house appeared freshly painted white with dark green shutters around the windows like the other farms he had passed. Uniformity. It was like that in Pennsylvania also.

A few things were different. The buggies here were black. Where he lived, in Lancaster County, the buggies were gray. He'd also noticed during the commute, as they arrived in Montgomery, that the women's prayer coverings were shaped differently, their dresses a bit longer than where he lived, and most of the men wore jeans, not slacks, but the denim pants didn't have back pockets.

Jeremiah knew from his travels that Amish districts, even ones within a few miles from his home, adhered to their own rules. They all had the same basic understanding of the Ordnung, but uniformity was key, no matter where one lived in an Amish community.

He set his suitcase off to one side of the porch before he knocked on her door, and she opened it holding Hank. Even with a screen door between them, it didn't alter his memory of her. She was more beautiful than he remembered with her sparkling hazel eyes and slightly taller than he'd recalled.

After gazing at her for too long, he dropped his eyes to the dog in her arms. "This is unbelievable." He shook his head as he gazed at Hank, then locked eyes with Ada. "I don't know how to thank you for tending to Hank. It was the happiest I've seen *mei mamm* since the accident."

He'd told her that on the phone, but the only other thing he could think to say was "You're beautiful," and that didn't seem appropriate.

"You're welcome." She scratched the dog behind one ear as she coddled him with one arm. "I have some medications I'd like to send with you. There are a few places that you still need to keep an eye on, and one spot on his nose that I've been trying to keep covered. Although he isn't fond of the bandage." She stopped scratching the dog's ears and pushed the screen slightly open. "Please come in."

Jeremiah was hit with the aroma of something heavenly, freshly baked or still in the oven, a hint of cinnamon in the air. He'd eaten at the airport before he'd taken the two-hour ride in the taxicab to get to Ada's house. But he would welcome a bite of whatever the smell represented, if offered.

He followed her to a mudroom that had been turned into a makeshift veterinarian office, complete with an examination table, shelves with bandages and medication, and two kennels.

She placed the dog on the examination table and began showing him where the animal still had remnants of the car crash. "These are the spots I've been keeping a close eye on for infection, but so far, so *gut.*" She met his eyes. "He loves to play fetch." She took a deep breath. "I'll send the tennis ball with you that I bought for him."

"*Ya*, great. I'll make sure he gets some playtime and exercise. He'll be *gut* company for me while I work on the *haus.*" He smiled at her, but she didn't return the gesture as she bagged up ointments and bandages.

Jeremiah picked up the dog, who growled. "Uh oh," he said.

Ada reached for the dog. "You can't hold him that way." She gently eased the dog out of his arms. "He is still tender right here." She maneuvered the animal slowly, and Jeremiah saw the remnants of what appeared to be a healing wound on his underbelly, still red with tufts of brown hair growing back and tiny holes where stitches had been. Looking back at him, she said, "I'm sorry if I sounded snappy. I should have been clearer when I was explaining and showing you his injuries."

She turned and walked briskly to the door, carrying Hank, without an offer of whatever aroma hung in the air.

Jeremiah had already formulated a makeshift plan of ways to spend more time with her during his stay, but the plan was unraveling as her curtness continued. When she practically shoved Hank into his arms, her action drove the point home.

"Best of luck to you, and again . . . my sympathies to you and your family." Then her eyes fixated on the dog. "Goodbye, Ollie . . . I mean, Hank."

Jeremiah assumed she had temporarily named the dog Ollie, but she closed the door without smiling or further conversation.

As he stared at the door that had practically slammed in his face, he glanced at his suitcase and wondered how far of a walk it was to Nellie and John's place. It couldn't be too far if Hank had made it here after the accident. He had hoped she would offer him a ride, part of his plan to spend time with her.

Sighing, he set the dog down on the porch and searched in the bag she gave him for a leash to attach to his collar, hoping the animal would be able to walk along beside him as he carried his suitcase.

Even though he had the address and directions to Nellie and John's house, it would have been nice to have a better understanding of the route. But Ada had been clear that she had been ready to get rid of the dog . . . and Jeremiah.

Before he could attach the leash to the collar, Hank scurried to the front door and began scratching against the screen.

"*Nee, nee,* Hank. Don't do that. You might rip her screen." Then the pup started to whine, and Jeremiah picked up the animal. Ada had been all he'd known for over a month. The poor fellow was probably having some separation anxiety.

He positioned the animal on his hip as best he could, then lifted his suitcase, hoping again that it wouldn't be too long of a hike. It had been a long day of travel already.

Ada had squeezed her eyes closed and covered her ears when she heard Ollie whimpering. Now, as she peeked out the window, she saw Ollie's sweet face looking back at her over Jeremiah's shoulder. Even though she didn't want to know Jeremiah any more than she already did — and she didn't want to say goodbye to Ollie again — what kind of person lets a man take off on foot carrying a dog and a suitcase? It was at least a mile to Nellie and John's house.

She rushed to the door, then sprinted down the porch steps. "Wait!"

Jeremiah spun around, smiling. *"Ya?"*

It was hard to let go of Ollie. She could do without Jeremiah's charming smile set against a seemingly naturally tanned face, home to dark brown eyes that Ada felt sure she could get lost in if she allowed herself. She motioned for him to come her way.

"Didn't you arrange for transportation?" Ada couldn't recall any mention of it during their brief couple of phone calls. She just assumed he had.

"Uh . . . *nee,*" he said as he grew closer to her. Then he startled and almost dropped his suitcase when Ollie wiggled out of his grasp, hit the ground with a yelp, then ran to Ada.

Her heart was cracking as she instinctively opened her arms and welcomed him back. "Silly boy," she said as she scooped him up.

"Hank is attached to you," Jeremiah said when he reached her. "I'm not surprised."

Ada hung on his words as she tried to decide if he was flirting with her. A part of her hoped so. The more logical side of herself refused to be lured in by a man who would be leaving in a couple of weeks. She'd already allowed a dog to control her emotions, which were beginning to spiral.

"His name is Ollie. He answers to Ollie now." She raised her chin and hugged the dog closer.

"Uh . . ." Jeremiah scratched his cheek, then tipped back the rim of his straw hat. "Okay."

"I mean . . ." Ada huffed. "I didn't know his name, so I just began calling him Ollie, and I think he's used to that." She forced her eyes away from him and focused on the dog in her arms, nuzzling his nose. "But he's your dog now, so I suppose you can call him whatever you'd like."

She looked at him in time to see him shrug. "I like the name Ollie. But I don't think it matters what we call him. He clearly adores you."

"I've had him for a while," she said, hoping she could keep her emotions in check. She cleared her throat. "You can't walk all the way to Nellie and John's *haus* toting a dog on your hip and carrying a suitcase."

He agreed. "It's a bit much to juggle."

Ada raised an eyebrow. "What if it had been raining? Or snowing?"

Smiling broader, he looked up at a clear blue sky, the sun full and radiant. "But it's not."

"I would think you would have planned better." Ada tried to say it with a hint of playfulness, but she didn't think it came out that way when he frowned.

"Do you have a driver I can call?" His charm peeled off right in front of her, and she realized her harsh tone must have turned him cold.

"I-I can take you and . . ." She slightly lifted the dog and raised her eyebrow again.

"I think we'll stick with Ollie," he said, still not smiling. "But I don't want to put you out."

"*Nee,* it's no trouble. I should have offered earlier." She tucked her chin until her cheek was next to Ollie's. "I'm sorry."

When she looked back at Jeremiah, he pointed over his shoulder. "If you'll allow me, I'll ready your horse and stash *mei* suitcase on the seat." His charm was re-emerging like fresh foliage on an early spring day, bright and welcoming. She liked him better this way even if it did cause her heart to flutter in an unfamiliar way.

She'd take him to Nellie and John's house, then say goodbye to him and Ollie for good.

CHAPTER 8

Jeremiah drove the buggy at Ada's insistence so that she could hold Ollie — as he was now named — after attaching a leash to his collar. The dog had made it clear that he was attached to this gorgeous woman in the passenger seat, but Jeremiah wondered how hard it was for Ada to give up the animal. Twice, he'd caught her lip tremble during the short commute, and by the time they reached the house, she had taken some sunglasses from her small handbag and was now hiding behind them. Please don't be crying.

He should have expected this since she'd had the dog over a month. And, as the resident vet, she loved animals. He should have planned transportation from Ada's house to Nellie and John's, but as part of his plan to spend time with her, he hadn't. Now, here he was with a woman and her dog, who didn't want to part ways with each other.

"Turn here," she said as she pointed to Nellie and John's house on the left.

"*Ya,* I remember." Memories began to regroup in his mind. No matter how he tried to organize his thoughts, sadness ruled. He already missed Nellie and John and the wonderful times he'd had with them. After he allowed his sadness to settle, he would be able to get to work on the repairs. But, right now, he couldn't seem to step out of the buggy.

After an awkward silence, she finally said, "Would you like for me to come in with you?"

He glanced in her direction, but with her sunglasses on, it was difficult to know if she pitied him, didn't want to leave the dog, or was genuinely trying to make things easier for him. Even though her giving him a ride was part of his plan to know her better, now he was worried himself about crying when he entered the house.

"I-I've already put you out enough." He tried to force a smile, then stepped out of the buggy and pulled his suitcase from the backseat. By the time he walked around to her side of the buggy, she had already stepped out and set the dog on the ground, grasping his leash. But she didn't hand it over to him, only shuffled to a dry patch of grass amid the gravel driveway. Jeremiah loosely tethered the horse to a fence post, unsure of her intentions.

She didn't say anything and waited patiently for Ollie to do his business before she put a hand to her forehead, still wearing her sunglasses, and stared at the white house which resembled a postcard with hues of orange and red against a blue sky in the background. Jeremiah took in the scene, as the homestead really was beautiful. To his left, a tire swing still hung from an oak tree, the same tire he used to spend hours on during his visits as a kid.

She turned to him, removed her sunglasses, and said, "I'll go in with you."

He was grateful, but still concerned about the knot that had formed in his throat. He nodded. *"Danki."*

Ollie trekked beside her with a bounce in his step as Ada and the dog led the way. She stepped aside when they reached the front door. Jeremiah set down the suitcase, then fumbled in a side pocket of his jacket until he pulled out a key and unlocked the front door. He hadn't realized until this moment how much he dreaded going inside the house, having to look for the things his mother wanted him to take home, and . . . having to do it alone.

The smell of stale air and the absence of daily life hung in the air as she followed Jeremiah into the house. "I'll open some windows," she said after unhooking Ollie's leash from his collar. Her precious pup wagged his tail as he ran from room to room, sniffing with familiarity his old home — a reminder that he wasn't her dog at all. He'd had owners, and now he would have new people to love him. Sighing, she lifted another window.

No matter her circumstances, and not wanting to say goodbye to the dog and the man again, it would have been cruel to let Jeremiah enter the home by himself when he was clearly emotional about it. But she also suspected that his lack of transportation might have been a way for him to spend more time with her, which seemed pointless since he wouldn't be here long.

Ada began in the living room, unlocking the windows and lifting them, allowing the cool breeze to waft inside. It was cool enough for a fire, but that would be counterproductive right now.

"I'll clean out these ashes in the fireplace." Jeremiah removed the screen and set it gently on the wood floors before reaching for the tools next to the fireplace. "*Danki,* again, for offering to come, um . . . inside. It's just . . ."

His voice cracked as he spoke, and his fumbling words tugged at her heart. He looked around, his expression that of a person caught in a turmoil he wasn't prepared for.

"I'll go find a garbage bag." Ada lifted the last window in the living room before she moved toward the kitchen. Her fireplace had a louvered grate to push ashes through to the outside. Apparently, Nellie and John's home did not, or else there were too many ashes to get to it.

"Danki," he said when she returned with a trash bag. His eyes, the ones she could lose herself in, were moist as he turned away from her.

"I saw a tub of butter on the counter." She cringed. "It had mold on it. If you'd like, I can clean up the kitchen and take inventory of what you might need while you're here." Despite her earlier resolve not to get close to Jeremiah, his semi-cheery disposition had shifted the moment they pulled into the driveway. She was doing what any friend would do, although they weren't really friends. Acquaintances. And that's all it would ever be.

"*Nee, nee.* I can't have you do that. You've already done too much. I'll get to that later." He shook his head, still not looking at her.

"I don't mind. I know you must be tired from your travels." She moved toward the kitchen, Ollie on her heels, before he could debate further. The man should at least have a clean kitchen, and from her experience, most men — her father included — couldn't make their way around a kitchen or know what was necessary to function in one. She took the last trash bag from the box in the pantry. She found a slip of paper and pen to start a list of what he might need, starting with garbage bags.

She took in a deep breath. Even though she hadn't known Nellie and John well, she pictured them sipping coffee at the small table with four chairs near the window. A cardinal peered at her through the dusty pane, and she momentarily pondered the significance. Her grandmother used to tell her that cardinals were spiritual birds, and that spotting one was a visitor from heaven. Was Nellie watching Ada's intrusion into her kitchen? Even though she wanted to help, it felt like a violation of privacy.

She opened the kitchen window, then noticed two bowls in an elevated tray on the floor with the name Hank written on both. The dog stood by the empty containers and peered up at her. It was the first time she thought about this as Ollie's domain, the reason he had jogged around the house comfortably when they arrived. This was his home. She filled up one of the bowls with water, but she hadn't found any dog food.

After she'd finished wiping down the counters, she inventoried the pantry, then walked back into the living room where Jeremiah was still shoveling ashes.

"I made a list of things you might need while you're here." She paused when he nodded. "I put coffee on the list. Do you drink coffee?"

"*Ya*," he said barely above a whisper.

"And I used your last trash bag to throw away some expired items that were in the pantry. They're on the list also. And you need dog food. I should have thought to send some."

"*Danki.*"

His voice cracked again, and Ada wasn't sure what to do. Did he want to be alone or have company? She glanced at Ollie, knowing it would be hard to leave him, but she was finding it difficult to walk away from Jeremiah, at least until she knew he was all right. This couldn't be easy for him.

Jeremiah placed the fireplace shovel back on the stand, straightened, and brushed his hands on his black trousers, leaving streaks of gray ash. He moved swiftly to the couch and grabbed a blanket. "You're shivering," he said as he bent down and draped it around her shoulders. She'd shed her black cape and bonnet when she'd first arrived and hadn't noticed the chill while she'd been moving around. He gingerly pulled the edges of the blanket beneath her chin, with his face entirely too close to hers, his dark eyes ablaze with what she could only identify as passion. She couldn't remember the last time she'd kissed a man. She didn't think that was part of Jeremiah's plan, but good sense told her to lean back in case her assumption about the look in his eyes was correct.

"*Danki,*" she said before forcing her eyes from his, unsure she'd ever felt such an immediate attraction to any man. And it wasn't just that she felt sorry for him, which she did, but there was something in his mannerisms, the way he carried himself, the deep voice, and those mysterious dark eyes that drew her to him. She wondered why he wasn't married, evident by his still clean-shaven face.

After he stood tall again, Ada rose from

the couch, feeling a blush on her cheeks as she recalled what she thought almost happened.

Jeremiah cleared his throat. "*Danki* for the ride." He took off his hat and set it on the tan couch before running a hand through his hair. "I guess I need to find some transportation while I'm here. I'm sure I'll need to go to the hardware store or lumberyard for supplies." He raised an eyebrow. "Unless they deliver?"

"I know you are only planning to be here a couple of weeks, *ya*?" He nodded. "I don't think either of the small stores in town deliver. You'd have to go to Bedford, and I suspect they would charge a hefty price. If it's something I can fit in *mei* buggy, I'd be happy to take you." *What am I doing?* She was doing exactly the opposite of what she'd planned.

"I've already put you out enough."

"It's no problem." Ada smiled, aware she was going down the rabbit hole.

She glanced at Ollie who had chosen a spot on a recliner across the room, then she walked toward him and squatted, giving him a scratch behind the ears. "Don't forget to change the bandage on his nose." She hated that her voice was shaky.

Her heart sunk a little. Ollie was home.

Would he even miss her? Probably not while he was staying in a familiar place. But what about when he left for Pennsylvania?

She forced herself to stand, looking over her shoulder twice at the dog. "Here's the list I made for you." She pulled the slip of paper with a grocery list out of her pocket. "Let me know if you need anything else during your stay here. And, as for your supper this evening, there are several jars of homemade soup in the pantry, and I even saw a jar of chow-chow."

Ada bit her lip and looked past him at Ollie again.

Jeremiah glanced at the dog before he looked back at her. Ada hoped she didn't cry. Ollie had slept in her bed ever since he had recovered enough to do so, and play time was every evening at five. He would round up his ball, wherever he'd hidden it in the house, then bring it to her.

"Uh . . ." He rubbed his chin as he scanned the list Ada had made for him. "I just thought about something. I don't have any dog food."

"I didn't find any in the cupboard, so I put that on the list. I didn't even think to bring any." She pressed a hand to her forehead.

Jeremiah yawned. "I'm going to impose

on you one more time."

Ada waited.

"I'm exhausted. I believe the *Englisch* call it jet lag. And since I don't have any food for Ollie, maybe you could keep him tonight."

Ada tried not to smile, but she squatted and called Ollie, who rushed to her right away.

She picked him up and put him in her arms, nuzzling his nose as the blanket fell from her shoulders. "I guess I can tolerate this little fellow another night." Ollie licked her face until she giggled. "Sweet boy."

"He sure does like you." Jeremiah picked up the blanket and placed it on the couch before he walked back to her.

"And I like him too." She gazed into Jeremiah's dark eyes for much too long. "It'll be dark soon. I best be going." But she didn't move.

Jeremiah didn't move either. And once again, she felt awkwardly close to his face, but in a way that sent warm shivers up her spine. When he reached for Ollie, he petted the dog on his head, then smiled.

"I'll go to the store tomorrow morning and get some dog food," he said. "I really should have thought about that."

She laughed. "How are you going to get there?"

He rolled his eyes and chuckled.

"I'll pick you up tomorrow morning. I know the ladies at the market, and Ollie will be fine riding in the basket."

"Are you sure?" He cringed. "I didn't plan very well."

"You've had a lot on your mind, I'm sure. I need to pick up a few things anyway at the store for myself."

"It's a date then."

Is it? She felt herself blushing again, "Um, okay, um . . . I'll see you tomorrow." She took Ollie and dashed for the door, giving a quick wave on her way out before her swirling emotions showed in her expression. This day hadn't gone according to plan.

CHAPTER 9

Jeremiah waved from the front porch following Ada and Ollie's speedy departure. Maybe he shouldn't have said that it was a date. He meant it to be playful but based on the way Ada had rushed out the door, it might have been a mistake.

But he was still feeling hopeful. Everything had gone according to his plan. Ada probably thought he was the most scatterbrained man she'd ever met by not arranging transportation during his stay. But how else was he going to spend time with her?

One thing was for sure. She loved that dog. *It is going to break her heart when I take him with me to Pennsylvania.* And maybe spending time with her and the dog would make it that much harder for her to separate from the animal when the time came, but he couldn't help himself. He'd been drawn to her since he'd first laid eyes on her during his last trip here, despite the circumstances.

He'd almost embarrassed himself earlier when he had let his emotions get the best of him. It was still hard to imagine that Nellie and John were really gone. Being at their home and among their belongings had both a strange calming effect on him, brought on by the familiarity, but also a sadness that lingered in his heart. He would never smell Nellie's fabulous baking or see her sweet smile. There would be no more trips to the barn to puff on a cigar with John, or sharing jokes and feeling like they were getting away with something. Jeremiah hadn't ever liked to smoke, not even the smell, but he would covet the special times with his uncle forever.

The exhaustion he'd told Ada about was real. He could barely keep his eyes open as he closed the windows. He made a fresh fire, and the house took on an entirely different smell with new cedar burning. He laid on the couch, unable to bring himself to sleep in Nellie and John's bed, the only bedroom downstairs. Upstairs would be freezing.

He pulled the blanket over him, the one he'd draped around Ada's shoulders. Bringing it up to his face, he breathed in the scent of her . . . of lavender.

Why isn't she married? Surely, she'd been courted. Perhaps, like him, she was just waiting for the right person?

Two or three weeks. That wasn't very long to get to know someone. But that was the agreement he and his father made, deciding that was ample time to do the repairs and get the house ready to sell.

His thoughts drifted back to his aunt and uncle, the loss heavy on his chest and in his heart. *And what about the dog?* How in the world did Hank — Ollie — survive the crash?

Jeremiah had been praying that God would heal his heart, wash away the grief that had stung so badly at first. His pain was still close to the surface, and he was acutely aware of the loss. But was the dog's survival part of God's perfect plan for him and Ada to get to know each other, or was he reading into it too much? Did Ollie survive to give comfort to his grieving mother?

Jeremiah had a niggling feeling that there was more to it. He hoped so.

Ada arrived home just before dark, and after a quick bite to eat — for her and Ollie — she doctored the dog's nose and showered, then they crawled in bed. Just like they'd been doing for over a month.

How was it going to feel when Jeremiah took Ollie away from her? She had expected today to be the day, and she'd prepared herself mentally. Then, a foreign personality had taken up residency in her mind and taken control of her speech. Being around Jeremiah had that bizarre effect on her.

She was doing everything she said she wouldn't do, but she couldn't be sorry right at this moment, not with Ollie curled up next to her.

After her nightly devotions, she snuggled beneath the covers as Ollie lightly snored, her mind filled with thoughts of Jeremiah, a man she barely knew. Would their new friendship change over the course of the next two weeks? If so, how hard would it be to say goodbye to him . . . and Ollie?

The next morning, Ada was glad for warmer temperatures but still chose her covered buggy for the commute to Jeremiah's house. There was still a chill in the air.

Ollie was content in the small kennel in the backseat, and when she pulled up to Jeremiah's house, he was standing on the front porch sipping from a coffee cup, wearing black slacks, a dark blue shirt with suspenders, a black coat, and topped off by his straw hat and a smile that warmed her insides.

He placed the cup atop a small table on the porch before trekking down the front steps.

"*Wie bischt,*" he said when he climbed into the buggy, still smiling, which only fueled her desire to know him better. After he was inside, he looked over his shoulder at Ollie. "*Wie bischt,* Ollie." The dog's ears perked up slightly, but he appeared otherwise uninterested.

"Do you have the list I made for you?" Ada asked, returning the smile.

He nodded. "*Ya,* I do, and I can't thank you enough for offering to take me shopping." He took a deep breath and blew it out slowly. "Bad planning on *mei* part." He grinned. "Can you rent buggies like the *Englisch* rent cars?"

Ada laughed. "*Nee,* I don't think so. Possibly you could borrow a buggy, but . . ." Her better judgment was gone. She'd just have to embrace her attraction to this man. "I don't mind taking you places. It's only for two weeks, and it's really no problem."

It was only a few minutes later that they were steadily on the road. "We're going to a small market that is run and visited mostly by our people. Occasionally, an *Englischer* will wander in, but mostly curiosity seekers about our way of life."

He nodded. "We have that back in Lancaster County, in Paradise where I live." He tipped his head in her direction and raised an eyebrow, something he did often, a quirkiness that made him even more attractive. "But you're lucky. This is a much smaller town and without the tourism where I live." He held up a palm. "Not that I can complain too much. The tourists drive our livelihood in a lot of ways, but the reason Nellie and John moved here was for less competition when it came to construction jobs and a quieter life overall. And, from what I heard, he was successful here."

"And he was well-respected," Ada said, trying to keep her attention on the road. "I heard he always quoted a fair price for a well-done job."

"Are your parents here? Do you have siblings?"

"*Mei* parents moved to Shipshewana about a year ago." She recalled the difficult decision to stay in Indiana. "We have relatives there, and I think *mei mamm* is just the opposite of Nellie and John. She craved the excitement of a bigger and more touristy area." She paused as she flicked the reigns to ease the horses into the entrance of the market. "But not me. I *lieb* it here, and I had already put a down payment on *mei haus*. They, *mei* parents, should be visiting soon, I hope." She missed her mother and father but talked to them often. "And I'm an only child." She glanced in his direction. "Did you say you're an only child?" She hadn't heard anyone mention whether Jeremiah had brothers or sisters.

He twisted his face into a frown. "*Ya,* no siblings." One side of his mouth curled into a half smile shortly afterward. "But I plan to have lots of *kinner* someday. It was lonely being an only child."

"I agree. About the loneliness and longing for a big family."

"Well, here we are." Ada rested the reins on the seat between them. "This is the market."

"Thank you for getting us here."

Ada held her breath as she heard the word *"us,"* which sounded more intimate than Jeremiah probably intended.

"I also appreciate the conversation along the way."

Ada enjoyed that part too. But before she could say so, Jeremiah stepped out of the buggy and tethered the horse, then reached into the backseat to retrieve Ollie. Ada bundled up in her black cape.

The dog yelped when Jeremiah eased him from the small carrier in the backseat which sent Ada's heart racing as she rushed around the buggy to where he stood with the dog in his arms, a blanket wrapped around him as he whimpered.

"Uh, oh." Jeremiah frowned. "Did I do something to hurt him or pick him up wrong again? Maybe he's not completely healed?"

"He might still be sore, but he should be fine." Ada reached out her arms, and the dog wiggled out of Jeremiah's arms and into hers, quietening right away. "Dr. Farley said he is healing nicely."

"He's attached to you," Jeremiah said, his deep voice taking on a hint that a gentle giant resided inside of this gorgeous man and kindness oozed in his words.

"Maybe," she said. "I've had him for a while. And, surprisingly, no one has brought any other animals for me to tend to, so *mei* attention has been solely on him."

Jeremiah opened the door for her and Ollie to enter the store, and after Ada placed the blanket in the grocery cart, she set Ollie on the plush surface. He stood on his back paws and rested his front paws on the rim of the cart, seemingly taking it all in. The store was full, but not packed like it was right before school let out in the afternoons. Mothers would rush in to make purchases before they picked up their children when the bell rang, which they could hear from the market.

"*Ach,* oh *nee.*" Ada's heart skipped a beat. Jeremiah put a hand on her arm, which would surely make things worse. "What's wrong?"

She nodded to her left. "That's Esther and Lizzie over there. Remember, I told you they were the town matchmakers. They are going to go wild when they see us together." She turned to him, feeling a rush of red vining up her neck to her cheeks. "Please just ignore their comments. They are well-meaning."

Jeremiah laughed. "You've said that before at The Peony Inn." He paused. "Ignore them?" He chuckled more. "*Nee,* I say we have some fun with them." He winked at her, which sent her stomach into a nervous swirl as she shook her head.

"I don't think that's a *gut* idea. You have no idea what they're capable of."

Over the years, Ada had witnessed some of the extremes the women had gone to in their effort to play matchmakers with unsuspecting couples the women thought belonged together. They'd even locked one man and woman in their basement until the couple realized they were meant for each other. She smiled on the inside, recalling how the couple ended up together, married, and had a family. But that didn't change what was on the horizon. *Complete and total embarrassment.*

Jeremiah tipped his straw hat at the two older women. Lizzie was the boisterous tiny woman, and Esther was the large and more docile co-owner of The Peony Inn. He'd only been around her a few times since she'd been under the weather when he was there.

"*Wie bischt,*" he said as they approached.

Lizzie grinned, raising her eyebrows. Her sister, Esther, just smiled.

"And what are the two of you doing out this morning?" Lizzie asked as she reached into the cart to pet Ollie. He coiled back at first, but then allowed her to scratch his head. There had to be some reserved trauma due to what the dog had been through.

"Uh . . ." Ada brushed away strands of strawberry-blonde hair. "I'm just helping Jeremiah get some supplies for his stay." She lowered her head before looking back up at the women. "I'm afraid there isn't much at

Nellie and John's *haus*."

Lizzie's expression fell, as if she was recalling the loss, but she snapped back quickly. "How nice of you to help Jeremiah, Ada." She batted her eyes in a way that left no doubt as to her hopes for the two of them.

"She's been great," Jeremiah said as he placed a hand on her back. Ada stiffened at the surprise contact, but there wasn't enough resistance for him to end the charade. He kept his hand on her back. "She inventoried the kitchen, helped me get the stale smell out of the *haus,* and offered to drive me around while I'm here."

Esther's smile broadened as she eyed Jeremiah's hand on Ada's back. "How kind of you," she said, echoing her sister's comment.

Ada hadn't shrugged him off, so he edged a little closer to her. He wasn't sure if her rigid stance was out of surprise or disapproval, but the feel of her next to him sent a welcomed shiver up his spine.

"It's no problem." Ada's expression was stiff, like her posture. Maybe she would reprimand him later, but it felt worth it to see Esther and Lizzie's satisfied expressions. If Jeremiah could get close to Ada for real, would she resist his efforts? Maybe she should. He'd only be here for a couple of weeks before he and Ollie left. But, for now, he was going to let this play out and see her reaction. He eased his arm around her shoulder and drew her even closer. Public affection was discouraged where he lived, and he assumed it probably was here as well. But . . .

"Ada is *wunderbaar.*" Jeremiah glanced at her, and she was looking down, appearing to stifle laughter as she pressed her lips together. She was aware what he was doing, just having fun with the matchmaking women. But would she continue to play along?

"*Ya,* she is." Lizzie batted her eyes at them both again. "Isn't it funny how a dog can bring two people together?" She pointed a crooked finger at him. "*Gott* works in mysterious, and sometimes, miraculous ways."

"*Ya,* He does." Jeremiah gave Ada a gentle squeeze. She was still looking down with her lips pressed together.

Lizzie lifted her tiny shoulders and grinned. "We will let you two get back to your shopping." She gave a little wave, and so did Esther before they disappeared around the corner.

Jeremiah and Ada were the only ones left near the entrance of the coffee aisle. And

Ollie was perched on his back legs looking around.

Ada twisted to face him, shaking his arm from around her shoulder, her lips still pursed together as she locked eyes with him. *Uh oh.* Maybe he'd misread what he'd thought was stifled laughter. Maybe she was angry.

He held his breath and waited for her to say something.

CHAPTER 10

Ada stared at Jeremiah and attempted to hold her firm expression, but he looked so forlorn that she burst out laughing instead, quickly covering her mouth with her hand to shush her giggles and hope he relaxed. "What in the world were you doing?" She said through muffled hands. She knew, of course, since he'd said he wanted to have some fun with Lizzie and Esther.

He shrugged with a cautious smile. "Just playing," he said softly in his deep voice as his eyebrows furrowed. "Maybe I went too far."

She laughed again. "You do know that by the end of the day, everyone in this town will think we're a couple? Lizzie and Esther know everyone, and they aren't shy, especially if they think they can take credit for two people, um . . ."

He stared at her for several long moments. "Why isn't someone as beautiful as you married?"

Ada's jaw dropped. She wasn't usually at a loss for words, but this direct personal question caught her off-guard as she pondered how to answer. The truth was always best, so she took a deep breath. "I guess I haven't found the right person." She folded her arms across her chest and raised her chin. "I suppose I could ask you the same thing."

He blew on his fingertips then rubbed them against his blue shirt that was peeking out from beneath his black jacket, and he winked at her. "You mean why isn't someone as handsome as me married yet?"

She bit her bottom lip and fought the grin that was coming through despite her efforts. "Handsome and . . ." She raised an eyebrow. "A tad arrogant, maybe?"

He pointed a finger at her. "So, you do think I'm handsome."

"Are you going to answer the question?" She reached out and gave Ollie a quick scratch behind his ears. "Why aren't you married?" Her heart was beating too fast as she waited for a response.

"Same as you. I haven't found the right person." He shrugged. "But I stay hopeful." He winked at her again. The man was playful, and she liked that.

"*Ach,* well, I guess we better get your groceries and —"

Ollie jumped out of the grocery cart, skidded down the aisle, and went straight for a woman about Lizzie's age who was holding a tiny little dog in her arms. He jumped up, nipping at the woman's dress as he growled at the Chihuahua in her arms.

"Ollie! *Nee!*" Ada was surprised at the dog's energy. She abandoned her cart and rushed to the woman, but Jeremiah darted past her and scooped up the dog, who was still growling.

"Lydia, I'm so sorry." Ada had known the elderly woman her entire life.

"What a vicious animal," the woman said, her voice cracking, as she clung to her dog.

"He's really not." Ada brought a hand to her chest as she eyed Lydia's dog. She had tended to the animal before when he'd had a cut on his foot. "I just think he isn't used to being around other animals."

"Ow!" Jeremiah held Ollie at arm's length as the dog twisted in his grasp. Blood dripped from Jeremiah's hand.

"Or people, apparently." Lydia took a step backward, pulling her Chihuahua closer.

Ada took Ollie from Jeremiah and got a good look at the bite on his thumb as they exchanged the pup. "I don't think he would have bitten you if not for the other dog."

"Blame it on my poor Lulu." Lydia huffed before she nodded to Jeremiah. "You best tend to that bite." She walked away shaking her head.

"Ollie, bad boy." Ada took a clean handkerchief from the pocket of her black apron and handed it to Jeremiah, who chuckled.

"That was surprising." He dabbed at the fresh wound on his right hand.

"Are you all right?" Ada set Ollie in the basket now that Lydia and her dog were out of sight and Ollie had stopped barking. She inched closer to Jeremiah and lifted his arm in her hands, then pulled back the handkerchief to inspect his hand. "You don't need stitches, but we're going to need to clean that up when we get home."

Jeremiah's eyes drifted to her hands holding his arm.

She eased away and stepped backward. "Let's get your supplies."

Jeremiah sat on Nellie and John's couch as Ada applied ointment and a bandage she'd found in the bathroom. He relished in the feel of her touch for a few moments before he glanced around Nellie and John's living room. So many memories. He had mixed feelings about his aunt and uncle's house.

In some ways, there was comfort in being at a place where they had lived and loved each other, but an overwhelming sadness still lingered around his heart when he thought about never seeing them again.

"Are you thinking about Nellie and John?" she asked.

"*Ya*, I guess I was." He gave his head a quick shake. "Sorry. Did you say something else?"

"*Nee*. You just looked like you were in a faraway place." She pulled the strip from the bandage and gingerly covered the small bite. Ollie was curled up in the same recliner as before.

"Memories." He tried to smile without much luck.

Her hand lingered atop his even after the bandage was on. "I-I guess I should be going." They'd unloaded the three bags of groceries, along with a bag of dog food, when they'd first arrived.

"Stay," he said softly, easing her hand back to his when she almost let go. "Just for a while?" He heard the neediness in his voice, and it was partly because he didn't want to be alone. But mostly, he didn't want her to go. Her presence soothed his soul, and the tenderness of her touch brought forth a longing he'd never had.

He waited, expecting her to deny his request. In some districts, it would be considered inappropriate for a single female and male to be under the same roof together. But they weren't teenagers. And, for Jeremiah . . . there was an air of danger in that fact. He was wildly attracted to her and reminded himself to be respectful of God's law when it came to intimacy.

"Okay," she said softly, leaving her hand in his, intertwining her fingers with his, almost unconsciously as she bit her lip and looked over his shoulder at Ollie. Maybe she agreed to stay because she didn't want to leave the dog.

Her eyes widened when she looked down and saw that they were holding hands. "*Ach,* sorry." She eased her hand away. "It's just been a . . ." She tipped her head to one side and grinned. "A strange day."

Jeremiah leaned back against the couch and kicked his socked feet up on the coffee table. Grinning, he shrugged. "*Ya,* I guess it has." He nudged her shoulder after she'd settled in beside him and kicked her socked feet on the table beside his. "Your dog bit me, and we're the talk of the town now, if you're right about Lizzie and Esther," he said, grinning. .

"*Ach,* I'm right." She laughed. "They're

at home planning our wedding."

Jeremiah felt an unexpected rush of warmth run through him even though the house was chilly. When Ada hugged herself and rubbed her arms, he could feel her shaking beside him. They'd both shed their outer garments when they walked into the kitchen, but now that they were still, the cool air was a reminder that spring wasn't here yet.

He reached for the blanket folded at the end of the couch, then wrapped it around her shoulders, lingering for longer than he should have. "There." He forced himself away from her and stood. "I'll get a fire going." He turned to her and scratched his cheek. "I didn't even ask if I'm keeping you from anything?"

She smiled and shook her head. *"Nee,"* she said sweetly.

Ada couldn't think of anywhere she'd rather be, and when Jeremiah returned to the couch, she laid her head on his shoulder. She'd never been this forward with any man she'd dated. Maybe it was because he was safe. She couldn't really lead him on since he would be gone in two weeks, and they both knew it.

He eased an arm around her shoulder. "Is

115

this okay?"

She didn't move her head from his shoulder when she nodded.

As Ada sat bundled next to Jeremiah, the fire crackled and popped. She closed her eyes, savoring the feel of him close to her, breathing in his scent, wishing she could bottle it to recall this moment in the future.

She startled when Ollie jumped down from the recliner and trotted his way across the room, then jumped into her lap. There was no growling this time, which confirmed for Ada that Ollie just wasn't fond of other dogs and wasn't aggressive with people under normal circumstances.

Jeremiah scratched behind the dog's ears. "He is a cutie."

Ada swallowed hard, reminded that her handsome new friend and her precious fur baby would be leaving in a couple of weeks.

A buzzing in Jeremiah's pocket took his arm from around her, and she lifted her head from his shoulder. "Sorry. *Mei mamm* said to leave *mei* phone on so she could reach me."

Ada listened. She could hear both sides of the conversation since Jeremiah was sitting so close to her.

"*Ya, ya.* Everything is fine. I hope *Daed* is doing okay without me there to help him,"

Jeremiah said.

"*Ya,* he is, but I know he'll be glad when you are home." His mother spoke to him tenderly, which reminded Ada that she needed to call her mother soon. It had been a few days, and sometimes just the sound of her mother's voice brought her comfort.

"Do I need to cut *mei* time here shorter?" He glanced at Ada, but she couldn't look at him as she hugged Ollie a little tighter.

"*Nee,* I don't think so. You probably scheduled the necessary time to make the repairs, and please don't forget to look for that box I was telling you about."

"*Ya, ya.* I will. You said you think it might be in the basement, right?" He scratched his chin, his arm brushing against her shoulder.

"I think so. Nellie told me she'd kept every letter John ever wrote her, along with keepsakes she treasured."

Ada heard the tremble in Lavina's voice, and she felt Jeremiah take a deep breath before he responded. "I'll find it, *Mamm.*"

His mother sounded like she was sniffling on the other end of the line. "Now, tell me about Hank. Nellie and John *liebed* him so much. It will be *wunderbaar* to have him here."

Jeremiah placed a hand on Ollie's back.

Ada wondered if they would call him Hank or Ollie.

"He's a cute fellow. He's sitting in Ada's lap right next to me."

There was a long silence before his mother spoke. "Um . . . Ada? Is that the woman we met at The Peony Inn?"

"*Ya,* I've inconvenienced her by not planning *mei* trip better. She took inventory of the kitchen yesterday, then took me in her buggy to the market and helped me get the things I need while I'm here. I didn't even have any dog food for . . ." He paused, glanced at Ada. ". . . for the dog."

His stumble caused Ada to wonder again if the precious dog in her lap would be called Hank or Ollie. Hank just didn't feel right, but that was the name he'd been given when Nellie and John had him. Ada hadn't known his name at the time, and to her, he still looked like Ollie.

"May I please speak to Ada?"

"*Ya,* okay." Jeremiah passed the cell phone to Ada with a slight shrug. "She wants to talk to you."

Ada put the phone to her ear. "*Wie bischt,* Lavina?"

"I just wanted to say *danki* for tending to Hank. It's such a miracle that he survived, and I can't wait to see him." Lavina paused, and Ollie licked Ada's hand as if the gesture would somehow soften the blow, a reminder that she couldn't keep the dog.

"You're very welcome," she said in a shaky voice she couldn't control, but she spoke softly so that maybe Lavina wouldn't hear her trembling.

"Jeremiah's father and I would like to pay you for tending to the animal. If you'll just let me know how much for your time and trouble, I will get the money to you."

Ada shook her head. "*Nee,* that's not necessary." She cleared her throat, hoping to clear the emotion in her voice. "It was a labor of *lieb.*"

"I think we still need to pay you something, but I will discuss it with *mei* husband."

"I really don't mind." She had to get off the phone before she burst into tears. "Once again, I'm sorry for your loss."

Ada handed the phone back to Jeremiah, stood abruptly, clutching the dog as the blanket fell from her shoulders. She quickly shuffled to the kitchen, Ollie in her arms.

Jeremiah said something to his mother that Ada couldn't make out before he ended the call. She was setting Ollie in front of his food and water bowls when Jeremiah entered the kitchen.

She slowly stood up and couldn't stop a tear from streaming down her cheek as her lip trembled.

"We have a problem, don't we?" Jeremiah pulled her into his arms and kissed her on the forehead.

His lips against her skin were like a gentle and comforting whisper that blended with the concern in his voice. She closed her eyes as a heady sensation threatened to overwhelm her, but she stayed in his strong arms, burying her face into his blue shirt and trying to stifle her cries. She was going to miss Ollie, but she was also basking in the tenderness she felt in Jeremiah's embrace. When she finally looked up at him, he gently took his thumb and wiped away her tears.

"I shouldn't have gotten so attached to him because I knew he might belong to someone else. But having him checked for a chip was the right thing to do." She didn't lift her head until he gently eased away from her. She straightened her lopsided prayer covering as Jeremiah brushed away loose strands of hair from her moist cheeks. His eyes locked with hers before he gently kissed her on the mouth, transporting her onto a soft and billowy cloud of euphoria.

Then he softly drew back, stopping, but

he continued to gaze into her eyes as if he was speaking to her, asking permission to continue.

Ada hadn't kissed a man in a long time, and the feel of his lips on hers sent a rush of longing cursing through her. He kissed her again . . . and again.

Then he stopped suddenly.

CHAPTER 11

Ada held her breath as Jeremiah took a step backward, his dark eyes sullen. He put a hand to his forehead. "*Ach,* I'm sorry. That was forward of me."

She wanted to tell him it was okay, that she'd enjoyed the kisses, but that also seemed much too forward, despite the closeness they had on the couch.

When she didn't say anything, Jeremiah stepped backward two more steps. He leaned against the kitchen counter and sighed. "I am wildly attracted to you, but that doesn't excuse my actions."

After she let the compliment soak in and fill her with warmth, it was time to let him off the hook. "It's okay. Really." Her stomach swirled with anticipation as she wondered if that would be enough for him to kiss her again. Hadn't she given him permission when she'd been so responsive earlier on the couch, putting her head on his shoulder?

"The problem is . . ." He ran a hand through his dark hair. "The problem is . . . geography." He nodded to Ollie. "And the dog."

Ada waited. Although she knew what he was going to say.

"Under different circumstances, I would want to court you, to get to know you better. I like you. I'm attracted to you." He paused as he locked eyes with her. "And I'll be leaving in a couple of weeks." He sighed again. "And taking the dog."

Ada lowered her head, staring at her socked feet. Ollie rubbed up against her, uninterested in his food or water. She finally looked up at Jeremiah. "I like you too." She pressed her lips together and tried to plan her words. "And I'm attracted to you also. But I'm aware that if we allow ourselves to become closer, there can only be heartache for one or both of us."

He looped his thumbs through his suspenders, any hint of playfulness gone. "*Ya,* exactly." He grinned. "But a person can never have too many friends."

She nodded, tempted to ask him if they would be able to be friends after both confessing their mutual attraction to each other. The intimacy they'd just shared felt like a lot more than friends, and she wondered how they could compartmentalize their feelings to make things convenient.

"Listen . . ." he said. "Would you want to help me look for that box of letters *mei mamm* was talking about?" He frowned. "It's not a task I'm looking forward to, but it seems important to *mei mamm*." His expression shifted into a mischievous grin "I'll keep *mei* distance."

Ada forced herself not to analyze their situation any further, She was glad the conversation had shifted and that it was playful. She grinned. "I'll hold you to that." Secretly, she hoped he wouldn't do as he said.

Jeremiah held a lantern and led the way down to the basement. "It's freezing down here." He turned to Ada over his shoulder. "Maybe you should stay upstairs, and hopefully, I can find the box quickly."

Ada wrapped herself more firmly in her black cape. "*Nee,* I'll be okay." She wasn't sure for how long. The lower they descended, the colder it became.

Jeremiah reached the bottom step, then twisted around and held the lantern for her to see. "Careful, it's a big final step."

After she'd landed beside him, he lifted

the lantern above his head and eyed the contents. There were two old rocking chairs, one lopsided with a broken leg, and the other was missing a slat on the back. There were boxes, most of them marked to identify the contents — Mamm's dishes, wedding memorabilia, school keepsakes, and other things that must have been important to Nellie and John. There were about ten boxes, and various other odds and ends were scattered about: an old mirror with a crack in it, a cedar chest, an old mattress and box springs, and a row of shelves with home-canned goods.

"We might want to pack up those jars. Nellie spent a lot of time on that, and even though I didn't know her well, I don't think she would want them to go to waste."

Jeremiah moved closer to the full shelves. "Do you want them?" he asked holding the light high and between them. "It looks like some pears, peaches, and pickles."

"Do you want to take them home?" Ada wasn't very good at canning, despite her mother's frequent attempts to show her how to do it correctly. She welcomed the gift.

"I'll take her a few jars since Nellie canned them. But *Mamm* has a basement full of food she has canned." He shrugged. "But I agree that they shouldn't go to waste. You should take what's left if you have room at your place."

"I'd be honored," she said softly.

Jeremiah sat on a stack of boxes and sighed. "Where to start?"

Ada carefully approached him, not wanting to get too close even though she longed for the warmth of his arms around her.

"Maybe the box marked wedding memorabilia?" That seemed plausible, but Jeremiah shook his head.

"*Nee, Mamm* told me before I left that it was a wooden box about the size of a shoe box, that Nellie had saved letters that she and John had written to each other when they were courting."

"That's so romantic." Ada felt herself blushing, thankful it was mostly dark in the frigid room. Then she saw something atop an old dresser in the corner. She pointed to her right. "Is that it?" A wooden box with a gold clasp was facing them.

"That's about how *Mamm* described it." Jeremiah moved in that direction.

When he reached the dresser, he brushed a plume of dust from the box, opened the clasp, and shone the light inside. Ada stood beside him, keeping her distance.

"I think this is it." He thumbed through the contents, mostly cards and letters. After he lifted it into his arms, he said, "Let's take it upstairs and get out of this cold basement. I'll pack up the canned goods for you later."

Ada wasn't going to argue. She was freezing and went directly to the fireplace after they reached the ground level. After she had warmed up, she warmed her hands, she removed her cape and hung it on the rack by the door. Jeremiah placed the box on the coffee table, then joined her by the fire and held his hands in front of the warm embers.

"We found that faster than I would have thought." He smiled.

Ada wondered if the comment was a hint for her to leave. Maybe he wanted to go through the box alone.

"Should we read the letters?" he asked, rubbing his hands together in front of the fire.

Ada shook her head. "*Nee*, that feels invasive." She brought a hand to her chest. "I mean, it's probably all right if you read them since you were close to your aunt and uncle, but I probably shouldn't." Although, she would love to read their correspondence and see how their love story unfolded.

Jeremiah cleared his throat. "I-I don't think Nellie and John would mind, but if you need to go —"

"I don't," she quickly said even though

hours had passed since their trip to the market, and this time of year dusk came early. "I'd just like to get home before dark." She paused. "If you really don't think they'd mind . . ." She bit her bottom lip.

Jeremiah put another log on the fire, then motioned for her to join him on the couch. Despite their earlier resolutions to keep their distance, his leg brushed against hers as they sat.

He took out the top item in the box. "Movie ticket stubs," he said before he chuckled. "I guess they enjoyed their *rumschpringe* like most teenagers."

He flipped through more of his aunt and uncle's memories, mostly tokens from places they traveled, a lot of postcards.

"They were quite the travelers," Ada said as she held up a postcard from Florida.

"I do recall that they traveled a lot, even when they lived back home." He paused. "Maybe it filled the void of them not being able to have *kinner.*"

Ada nodded. She wondered if she would ever have children. Not unless she found the right husband, and most folks in her community hoped for women her age to be in the family way sooner rather than later. Otherwise, she'd be thought of as an old maid if she was too late into her twenties.

Her eyes drifted in Jeremiah's direction as she briefly envisioned what their children would look like. Would they have strawberry-blonde hair like her, or would Jeremiah's dark hair be dominant? She snapped herself back to reality. Thinking of such things could only hurt her, and she barely knew the man.

"I don't see a bunch of actual letters, but here's one." Jeremiah pulled back the flap, hesitated, then took out a piece of yellowed paper. "Should we?"

"I don't know. It's up to you." She was in the mood to listen to a love letter, but Jeremiah was close to this couple. Would it be hard for him to read?

He sat quietly with the paper folded in his hand. Then he slipped it back in the envelope and rummaged through the other contents. Only postcards without anything written on the back, more movie stubs, a couple of concert stubs, and other various memorabilia.

He picked up the letter again, staring at it. "This is the only letter I see. I'm not sure why *mei mamm* would want this stuff, but if it's just this one letter, I say we read it. I don't think Nellie and John would mind." Jeremiah glanced her way as if he was seeking permission.

"Like I said, it's up to you." Ada gazed into his eyes and was pretty sure they were having a moment, mutual thoughts of kissing. She quickly looked away and stared at her lap.

Jeremiah took the letter from the envelope and unfolded it. "Will you read it aloud?"

"*Ya,* sure." She took it from him wondering if he might be worried about reacting emotionally to the contents.

Here goes . . . Ada took a deep breath before she began.

"Dear Nellie, I'm sad to be away from you, but the short time we had together keeps my memories alive with thoughts of you. When I feel lonely out here in Louisiana at the job site, I recall holding you in *mei* arms, kissing you . . ." She glanced at Jeremiah who had his eyes on her, not the letter. She cleared her throat. ". . . and I need to know if you feel the same way I do, if you think of me often and fondly.

"I don't understand why *Gott* would send me so far away from you if we were destined to be together. But He whispered in *mei* ear that I should tell you how I feel even though our romance was brief. I *lieb* you. I've *liebed* you since the first time I saw you at The Peony Inn."

Ada gasped as her eyes locked in surprise

with Jeremiah's. There were no words needed, so she continued to read.

"You were in the dining room, standing near the grandfather clock, and I'd never seen such a beautiful woman."

Ada could feel Jeremiah's eyes on her, and she wondered if this was God at work right now. She continued reading.

"If the ladies at the inn hadn't given us a nudge toward romance, maybe I wouldn't have had the nerve to court you."

Ada chuckled as she looked at Jeremiah. "See, I told you. Lizzie and Esther have been playing matchmakers for a long time."

Jeremiah didn't say anything, and she couldn't read his expression. She cleared her throat again and continued with the next lines.

"I *lieb* you, Nellie. I'm sure of it. I want you to know that, and I hope to hold you in *mei* arms again soon. All my *lieb,* John."

Ada swallowed back a lump in her throat. "I wonder how long they were away from each other."

Jeremiah stood, then began pacing the room. "Almost a year," he said before he turned to stoke the fire. "I wonder if he would have returned earlier if he'd known their lives together would be cut so short. Nellie was only ten years older than . . .

me." His voice cracked, and Ada instinctively rose and went to his side. She put an arm on his back, the feel of his muscles beneath her hand.

He turned to her, cupped both her cheeks, and slowly leaned in to kiss her, and she responded to his exploratory passion.

It was a mistake, but it was the most enjoyable mistake Ada had ever experienced.

Chapter 12

Over the next two weeks, Ada was with Jeremiah every day, carting him to town for supplies and often helping him with repair projects. She cleaned a lot even though he had told her not to do that. But the house needed to be spotless before the realtor listed it for sale.

Each night they ended the day with a meal that Ada prepared, and then they retired to the living room for devotions. And there were stories they told each other about how they grew up, funny things that had happened to them in life, precious moments they cherished. And there was always kissing with each nightly encounter becoming more passionate and intense.

Friendship was something they'd committed to in the beginning, but they'd both stepped outside that safe circle. Ada was in love with both the man and the dog. How could she possibly tell them both goodbye tomorrow?

Ollie was always in Ada's lap, and each night he went home with her before dark and slept in her bed. Jeremiah had insisted on it because the dog whimpered if she tried to leave without him.

On this last night that they would spend together, Ada fought tears throughout supper, and after not being able to focus during devotions, she hoped she could get through the goodbyes without an onslaught of sobs.

Jeremiah latched onto her hand as they sat on the couch, Ollie in her lap, glancing back and forth between them as if he knew what was happening.

"I can't take Ollie from you," he said softly as he petted the dog's back with his free hand. "You have become his owner, and he *liebs* you."

At first Ada's heart rejoiced at the thought of at least being able to keep Ollie, but then she thought about Jeremiah's mother, Lavina, and how much she was looking forward to having Nellie and John's dog. "*Nee,* it wouldn't be right."

"I'm going to talk to *mei mamm* about it." He spoke with an authority that Ada hadn't previously heard from him, as if the matter were settled.

"*Nee,* Jeremiah. Please don't. Your family has suffered a tremendous loss, and if Ollie — or maybe you will all decide to call him Hank — can bring even a little bit of comfort, a connection to Nellie and John, then he should be with you and your family."

Ada was proud of herself for getting the words out without crying, although her lip trembled now. And, coming soon, and equally as bad — actually, worse — she would be saying goodbye to Jeremiah. He had a driver picking him up early the next morning.

Still holding her hand, he looked at Ollie in her lap and smiled. "He looks like an Ollie to me." Then he tenderly cradled Ada's chin in his hand and gently turned her to face him. "I don't know how to thank you for everything you've done, and . . ." He paused. "I don't know how to say goodbye to you."

Just hearing the word 'goodbye' caused a frenzy of emotion to churn in her stomach. He kissed her softly on the mouth, and Ada was sure her heart was breaking.

"It's going to be dark soon." She might as well get this over with, and after letting go of Jeremiah's hand, she stood, walked to the recliner, and eased Ollie into his favorite spot in the house. Even though he'd spent his nights with Ada, the familiar recliner had reconnected him to his former home during the days. Then she leaned down, kissed the dog on the forehead, and through tears, she said, "I will miss you, Ollie, but you will have a new home with people who will *lieb* you the way I have . . . and the way Nellie and John did." She straightened, brushed the wrinkles from her black apron, and when she turned around, Jeremiah was standing in front of her.

He held her cheeks between both hands, kissed her with all the passion that had been building over the past couple of weeks, and with their bodies pressed together, it felt as if their hearts were beating as one.

"I have to go." She eased out of his embrace and glanced out the window. "It will be dark soon."

Jeremiah lowered his head and sighed before he looked back up at her. "I'd like to write to you if that's all right."

A part of Ada just wanted him out of her life so her broken heart would heal, but she said, "I'd like that." Never hearing from him again sounded worse.

He walked her to the door, and after another long kiss, she said the words she'd been dreading. "Goodbye, Jeremiah. And safe travels."

Jeremiah rarely cried. Even at John and Nellie's funeral, he had managed to keep his emotions in check for his mother's sake. But after Ada descended the porch steps, rushed to her buggy, and didn't look at him, his mind burned with the memories they'd made in such a short time. As she backed up, flicked the reins, and made her way to the road, he swiped at his eyes.

Ollie left the comfort of his recliner. jumped up on the couch, and propped his front paws on the back of the cushion. As he stared out the window, he whimpered.

Jeremiah lifted the dog into his arms. "I know, fella. Mei heart is breaking too."

Since Ada had told him that Ollie slept in her bed each night, Jeremiah carried the dog to his bed and patted the extra pillow. "Get comfy while I go take a shower."

After he was done, he exited the bathroom, and Ollie wasn't on the end of the bed. He walked into the living room, and the brown, white, and black bundle of fur was on the couch, his front paws propped on the back cushions as he looked out into a star-filled night, whimpering again for the loss of his beloved Ada.

Jeremiah glanced around the house and tried to picture someone besides Nellie and John living here. Their home was steeped with memories, but as he visualized his aunt and uncle carrying on with their daily chores, sharing meals, and the laughter Nellie was known for, he wished his parents hadn't decided to sell the home. But he also knew that, financially, it was necessary. And if no one was here on a regular basis, the house would fall into disrepair.

He picked up a reluctant Ollie, who squirmed in his arms, but when Jeremiah climbed into bed with the dog, the pup began to settle next to him.

Jeremiah pictured the look on Ada's face when she'd told them both goodbye, then he glanced at the clock on the nightstand. His parents might already be in bed, but his mother was most-likely still up reading a book.

He took his cell phone from beside him and dialed his parents' number. Life regarding cell phones would go back to normal when he returned — for use in emergencies or job-related calls — but this conversation couldn't wait.

"Jeremiah, is everything okay?" his mother asked when she answered, concern in her voice.

"*Ya,* I was just letting you know that I have a driver scheduled, and everything is going according to plan. I should be home tomorrow evening. It's an eleven-hour drive, plus any stops we make."

"Your *daed* and I are grateful for all you did to ready the *haus* for sale. I don't think I could have coped with that."

"I reserved a driver with a van to accommodate the things on your list that you wanted me to bring home. And I have the box you wanted."

"What box?" his mother asked.

"The one you said had letters and memorabilia. I found it in the basement."

"Oh." She was quiet. "Did you look at what was inside?"

He took a couple of moments before he answered. "*Ya,* I did. I hope that's okay." Cringing, he hoped for a positive reaction.

"*Ya,* of course. I know how much you *liebed* Nellie and John."

He scratched his cheek. "But *Mamm,* it was mostly postcards and ticket stubs, and various other keepsakes. The letters you talked about . . . there was only one."

"And you read it?" she quickly asked.

Guilt coursed through him despite her earlier comment. "*Ya,* I did. It was very touching."

His mother was quiet, and Jeremiah decided to get to the point of his call.

"It was hard to watch Ada saying goodbye to Ollie . . . I mean Hank. She named him Ollie before she knew who he belonged to." He swallowed hard, recalling how heartbreaking it was for him to tell the woman he'd fallen in love with goodbye.

"I'm sure it was difficult for her. *Gott* bless her for everything she did to nurse him back to health. One of *Gott's* true miracles that the dog survived."

"Um . . . *ya,* it really is. He's having some anxiety now that she's gone." He reached over and scratched Ollie's head. If dogs had expressions, Ollie's said that he was brokenhearted. His eyes darted around the room as if he expected Ada to walk into the room any moment. Jeremiah allowed himself to think about her in bed next to him but forced the thought away. He needed to stay focused on his mission. "Anyway, he really misses her, and I know how badly she is going to miss him. They were together for almost two months. He even slept in her bed."

He waited, hoping his mother would pick up on what he was saying and tell him to leave the dog with Ada.

"As I mentioned before, I plan to mail

Ada a check for everything she did."

Jeremiah was sure Ada didn't care about being compensated. She just wanted the dog. "I don't think she cares about the money, *Mamm*."

"*Ya,* well . . . I'm going to send her a payment in the mail. I know it won't ease the separation anxiety she must be having, but as a single woman, she must make a living."

Jeremiah recalled the three times when Ada had excused herself from helping him at the house to go tend to injured animals in their community. He didn't know until then that she made house calls when necessary.

He picked up on his mother's compassion. She knew Ada was having a hard time letting Ollie go. As much as he didn't want to hurt or take anything away from his mother, he wanted Ollie to stay with Ada.

He opened his mouth to tell her that, but his mother spoke first.

"I've been told that dogs travel best in a car when they are in a carrier. Do you have one for Hank?"

So far, his mother hadn't bent on the name, and she didn't seem like she was going to give up the dog. "*Ya,* Ada gave me an extra one she had," he said, defeated. But he couldn't deprive his mother of the one thing that she'd said would give her some peace — Nellie and John's dog.

"From your previous calls, it sounds like you spent a lot of time with Ada."

"*Ya,* I have. She helped a lot."

Silence as Jeremiah swallowed back the large knot in his throat.

"It must be hard to leave her. Such a beautiful woman." There was sympathy in his mother's voice.

If you only knew. "*Ya,* but I suspect we will remain friends since we agreed to write to each other."

"That's nice." His mother yawned. "A person can never have too many friends."

Jeremiah took a deep breath. He was going to have to come out and ask her if Ollie could stay with Ada.

"I can't wait to hold that little dog in *mei* arms. It will be special for me, like a part of Nellie in a way."

Jeremiah glanced at Ollie, then hung his head. There was no way he could deny his mother the one thing that would help soothe her soul.

"Good night, *Mamm.* Ollie and I will see you tomorrow evening."

"Good night, Jeremiah."

CHAPTER 13

Ada arrived at The Peony Inn for a quilting party that would be starting soon, toting a blueberry cobbler with her. As she walked up the porch steps, she saw Lizzie and Esther through the kitchen window. They were both sitting at the kitchen table. Ada tapped on the door and entered through the side entrance. *"Wie bischt,"* she said as she placed the cobbler on the table amid many other snack trays, jellies and jams, Lizzie's famous chow-chow, and a deli tray with various sliced breads. "Am I the first one here?" she asked the women.

"Ya." Lizzie scowled. "Have a seat."

Ada did as she was instructed. That was best when it came to Lizzie. "What's wrong?" Ada's stomach twisted.

"Esther and I don't understand how you let that man get away — Jeremiah. The two of you were clearly smitten with each other." Lizzie raised her palms in the air. "Have you even talked to him since he left?"

"*Ya,* I have." Ada raised her chin. "We've talked several times. Ollie is having a hard time adjusting to his new home, but he will get comfortable eventually." She took a deep breath. "As far as letting Jeremiah get away, the man had a home and a job to return to."

Ada had cried herself to sleep many nights, missing Ollie and Jeremiah. Sometimes, when Jeremiah called, she could barely contain her emotions. He'd been very sweet during every conversation, but they were both holding back for the good of the situation, Ada thought. They both admitted to cell phone abuse since there were no emergencies or job-related issues to justify the calls, unless you included Ada's inquiries about Ollie. But it would have felt impossible not to talk, at the least.

"*Ach,* well . . . John and Nellie's *haus* sold, so maybe he will be coming back to sign the papers." Lizzie pointed a finger at her. "Then you better latch on to that handsome fellow. You aren't getting any younger."

Lizzie's older and quieter sister, Esther, cleared her throat. "I heard from Marge, the *Englisch* woman that listed the *haus,* and she said that most closings are done with some type of digital signature, so it's unlikely Jeremiah will have to come back for that."

"I'll talk to Marge and tell her to make it mandatory for him to come sign the papers in person."

Ada's jaw dropped. She was still wrapping her mind around the fact that the house had sold, leaving a certain finality in its wake. "Lizzie, you will do no such thing!" She was surprised at the anger that came out when she spoke.

Lizzie rolled her lip into a pout. "I'm just trying to make sure you don't end up an old maid."

Esther sighed. "*Ach,* Lizzie . . . leave the child alone. She's hardly an old maid."

Lizzie huffed. "We are out of eligible bachelors around here. One pops into town, and you let him get away." She pointed a crooked finger at Ada. "And I happen to know that you spent a lot of time with that man while he was here."

Ada folded her arms across her chest. "And how would you know that?"

"I have *mei* sources."

"Who bought the *haus*?" Ada asked as she twirled the string on her prayer covering. Before she had met Jeremiah, she might have been hoping for a single man to purchase the farm. But no one would sway her feelings at this point.

"A family with one *kind*," Esther responded while Lizzie continued to pout. "That's all I know."

Thankfully, two buggies pulled up, and Ada could put an end to this conversation before Lizzie or Esther grilled her anymore about Jeremiah. She stood and uncovered her cobbler just as she heard voices from women crossing through the yard on the way to the house.

The conversation might have been over, but the hole in Ada's heart grew larger.

Jeremiah stared at the wooden box still sitting on the hutch in the living room where he'd left it before he slipped into his boots by the front door, then put on his hat. He was glad the temperatures had warmed up and spring was on the horizon, but something was bugging him.

When his mother walked into the living room, flour smudges on her black apron from early morning baking, he said, "Have you even looked in that box?" He pointed to the wooden box he'd brought from Nellie and John's house. Jeremiah had seen her going through a few other things he'd brought home a few weeks ago, but he was unsure if she had even touched the box.

"Uh . . ." His mother stopped, glanced at the box, then shrugged. "*Nee,* I haven't." She raised an eyebrow. "Have you?"

Jeremiah glanced out the window over his shoulder, knowing his father was waiting for him in the workshop. He hesitated. It had felt like a violation at the time, and even more so now. He lowered his gaze and sighed. "I already told you that I looked through it in Indiana. You said Nellie and John wouldn't mind."

"Did you find anything special?"

He slipped on his straw hat he was holding, then tipped the rim down so he didn't have to look directly at his mother. "*Mamm,* I already told you. A lot of postcards, some ticket stubs . . . things like that."

His mother tapped a finger to her chin. "What about the letter from John to Nellie?"

Jeremiah raised his eyes to his mother. He wasn't sure why she was questioning him this way. "It was very sweet." He paused when his mother smiled. "You seemed so intent that I did not forget that box. You asked me about it several times. I'm surprised you haven't gone through it, but it sounds like you might be familiar with the contents?"

"*Ya,* I am. Nellie showed me the note

right after she received it from John."

He wasn't sure where this conversation was going. "*Mamm,* I gotta go." Jeremiah glanced over his shoulder again. "*Daed's* waiting."

Ollie walked into the living room. Jeremiah was glad his mother had chosen to go with Ollie as a name for the dog instead of Hank. She reached down and picked him up. Ollie licked her face, the same way he used to do with Ada. Thoughts of her stayed with him. They broke the rules and talked often on the phone, but it was always guarded, as if they both knew it was something special that couldn't be.

"Your dad can wait a few more minutes." His mother nuzzled the dog, then set him on the couch where he settled onto a blanket that he had claimed.

"Where's Buster?" Their Blue Heeler was mostly his father's dog, and the animal hadn't been happy to share space with a new furry family member.

His mother sighed. "Out in the workshop with your *daed.*" She glanced at Ollie. "It's just taking some time for Buster to accept Ollie." She smiled as she glanced at the dog. "But I can see why Nellie *liebed* this fellow so much. He's a cuddler with a very sweet nature." She waved a dismissive hand.

"Anyway . . ." She took a few steps closer to Jeremiah and put a hand on his arm. "I want to tell you something. What you do with the information is up to you."

Jeremiah pushed back the rim of his hat and finally looked directly at his mother. "What's that?"

His mother blinked a few times as her eyes grew moist. This was going to be about Nellie. She took on a familiar expression when she had recollections of her sister. "I remember the exact moment when Nellie fell in *lieb* with John at The Peony Inn. She was standing by the grandfather clock, much the same way Ada was standing when I caught you two gazing at each other." She paused, her hand still on his arm. "*Sohn*, I've never seen you look at another woman that way. *Ya*, I've never been on your dates with you, but it doesn't seem like anyone has captured your interest the way Ada has."

Jeremiah couldn't agree more. "*Mamm*, even if that were the case, I have a *haus* and a job here. She has a *haus* and a great community where she lives. It's just not geographically possible for us to share a life together." Just saying the words aloud caused his heart to crack even more.

"That's what John and Nellie thought in the beginning." She smiled at Ollie. "*Gott* often has a way of turning tragedy into *gut*. If sweet Ollie hadn't survived, you probably wouldn't have spent so much time with Ada. And the way you've been moping around since you returned home tells me that you miss her."

Jeremiah wasn't sure how much to admit to his mother. He'd also thought about the miraculous scenario that had unfolded, but in the end, it had left him miserable. He was pretty sure Ada felt the same way based on their phone conversations, not to mention recollections of the memorable time they'd shared. He had allowed himself to dream about a life with her.

"You wanted me to read that letter. That's why the box was so important to you." Jeremiah swallowed back the emotion that was building. "I don't understand how it can help me."

"Then I'll tell you." His mother raised her other arm until she was latching on to both his shoulders, then she looked up at him with tears in her eyes. "I wanted you to see that all things are possible when you draw on the strength of Christ. And when *Gott* opens a door, it's almost always a path that He has chosen for you. *Sohn* . . . life is short." She paused, sniffling. "I don't want you to waste a minute of yours."

"*Mamm,* I *lieb* you, and I can see where you are going with this." He sighed as he lifted his shoulders and lowered them slowly as his mother dropped her arms to her side. "But it's an impossible situation."

She smiled. "Nothing is impossible."

CHAPTER 14

It was a few weeks later when Ada agreed to take Lizzie and Esther to the market, citing the possibility of rain and that they didn't see well in the rain. When Lizzie asked Ada to turn the buggy on the road that led to Nellie and John's old house, Ada suspected the women had ulterior motives. The word around town was that the new owners were moving in today, and there wasn't a cloud in the sky.

"I can't wait to meet the new members of our community," Lizzie said from the backseat of Ada's buggy.

Ada chuckled. "I didn't think there was rain in the forecast. You just wanted to see who our new neighbors are." She wasn't sure why they needed her to cart them around.

"It's always exciting when we have new members in our district." Esther rode up front with Ada. "I brought sugar cookies and a rhubarb pie."

"So, that's what is in the basket beside you, Lizzie?" Ada glanced over her shoulder and smiled. The sisters were beloved by everyone in their community. "Why didn't you ladies just tell me you wanted to meet the neighbors? I'd like to see who is moving in too."

"I hope it's a tall handsome hunk for Ada," Lizzie said with such excitement that Ada chuckled. Ada's heart was spoken for even if the recipient of her affections didn't know it and was unavailable. They'd continued to talk on the phone, and sometimes she could hear Ollie barking in the background, which tore at her heart. But it was the sound of Jeremiah's voice that dug deep into her soul.

"We already heard that it was a family with one *kind*." Ada shook her head. "I don't think he will be old enough to date."

"You never know," Esther said as she shrugged.

"The moving truck is here." Lizzie leaned forward between Ada and Esther. "See, I was right about the day."

Ada pulled back on the reins until her horse came to a complete stop. "I feel like we're intruding. These people are just now moving in. I'm sure they are weary travelers and not in the mood for company."

"Everyone is in the mood for Esther's baked goods," Lizzie said. "And I baked two loaves of bread, banana and pumpernickel, this morning. They're in the basket also."

Ada sighed. "If I had known . . ." She scowled at Lizzie over her shoulder, then at Esther. "I could have brought something, too, but I still think our visit is premature."

"Nonsense. They have to eat." Lizzie stepped out of the buggy carting the oversized picnic basket with the energy of someone half her age. "Let's go, let's go."

Esther was a little slower, and Ada took her time. Together they walked across the yard toward Nellie and John's old house. It was hard to picture someone else living there as she recalled all the work she and Jeremiah had done to the place. She knew she should be happy for Jeremiah's family, that the homestead sold so quickly, and that a new family would be living there. But it felt odd to her as she approached the porch steps. And when Lizzie knocked loudly on the door — Ada and Esther on either side — recollections of her time kissing Jeremiah flooded her mind and crushed her heart. Phone calls couldn't cure what ailed Ada.

"Here." Lizzie set the basket at Ada's feet. "You give them the food." Then she darted down the porch steps, Esther following as quickly as she could until they were both out in the yard.

"What are you doing?" Ada turned around, slammed her hands to her hips, and sneered. "Silly women. Get back here."

When the wooden door opened, she recognized the face on the other side of the screen. Jeremiah smiled broadly before he pushed the screen door open, careful not to knock her in the face, which surely showed the shock she felt as her jaw dropped.

"What are you doing here?" Ada almost jumped into his arms but held back since they had two sets of eyes on them. She assumed his parents were inside also.

"Surprise," he said, a huge smile on his face as he winked at her. "Those two were in on it and made me promise not to tell." He pointed past Ada at Lizzie and Esther, who grinned and snickered. Lizzie covered her mouth with her hands as she jumped up on her toes repeatedly.

"I-I don't understand." Ada brought a hand to her chest, hoping to slow her racing heart. "I thought a family bought the *haus*. Did you buy it?" She was afraid to be that hopeful. There had to be another explanation.

"A family did buy the *haus*." He grinned.

"*Mei* family."

Ada realized she must have looked like a fish out of water with her mouth still hanging open. She forced it closed, chewed on her lip, then grinned. "A family with one *kind.*"

"That would be me." He inched toward her.

"Where are your parents?" She leaned to the left so she could see around him, but she didn't hear any movement.

"They aren't here. They considered moving, but *mei daed's* business is there, and they have friends there."

The more he smiled, the more she wanted to jump into his arms. "I still don't understand," she repeated.

"As it turns out, *mei* Uncle John had a lucrative business here, and *mei* parents thought I should come here and run it. I sold *mei haus* and used it to buy this *haus. Daed* found someone to replace me, to help him with his construction business."

"*Ach,* that's *wunderbaar* that the business was so successful that it enticed you to live here." She hung on his words, still unsure if his motivation to move was solely business related. "I'm sure they're going to miss you."

"Maybe they will. I will miss them."

Her heart raced as he took a step toward her. "Do you really think that my uncle's business is the only reason I chose to make this move?"

Ada's heart pounded harder in her chest, especially when he closed the gap between them, the smell of his musky soap swirling around her and igniting all her senses in a familiar way. "I don't know," she said.

"Kiss her!"

Ada swung around to see Esther giggling and Lizzie — who had yelled at them — bouncing up and down.

Jeremiah held her cheeks tenderly. "I learned in *mei* short time here that it's best to do as Lizzie says. She can be a little bossy."

"I heard that!"

Ada smiled. *Could this really be happening?*

Then he did. Jeremiah leaned into her lips with all the passion she remembered. "I *lieb* you, Ada. I've *liebed* you from the first moment I saw you. But *lieb* runs deeper than one's own feelings, and *mei mamm* is a wise woman. I was miserable without you, and she wants me to be happy. Does *mei* being here make you happy?"

"More than anything," she said as her eyes grew moist. "And I *lieb* you too."

Jeremiah's expression shifted as he eased away from her and scratched his cheek. "Something is missing."

Ada's heart sunk. Had she not responded the way he wanted her to?

"I'll be right back."

She didn't understand why he didn't invite her in. Maybe he wanted to wait until everything was in order. Her chest tightened, her heart still beating much too fast. Then, she heard a rustling, followed by a familiar sound, and she gasped when Ollie came into view.

Ada knelt so the dog could jump in her arms, and there was no stopping the tears now. "*Ach, mei* sweet boy." She laughed as he covered her in wet kisses. "I have missed you."

She picked up her beloved Ollie, who had gained a few pounds. "But what about your *mamm*? I thought Ollie brought her comfort?"

"*Mamm* loved Ollie, but *mei Daed's* dog, Buster, wasn't having any part of it. She also knew how hard it was for you to say goodbye to Ollie, and she wanted you to have him."

Ada tried to speak, but she was too choked up to find the words, and Ollie kept kissing her as if he'd missed her as much as she'd missed him.

"*Mamm* knew that me living in Nellie and John's *haus* was like having a part of them still with us." He smiled, scratching Ollie's ears. "Save some of those kisses for me," he said to the dog before laughing.

Ada's heart was full. Esther and Lizzie clapped from their spot in the yard.

Jeremiah continued to pet Ollie. "*Gott* uses all things for *gut* — even a tragic accident. Without this fellow, we wouldn't have spent all that time together and gotten to know each other." "*Gott* is *gut*."

Ada smiled. "Every day."

Epilogue

Ada kissed her husband goodbye before leaving to go to work, although caring for animals in her former home didn't feel like work at all.

Jeremiah had proposed six months after his return, and they'd renovated Ada's smaller house into a veterinarian's office and shelter for homeless animals. Ada still cared for animals when she could, but she hired someone with an animal science degree as an assistant technician. The folks in her community had been leery of her English employee at first, but Ada paved the way. The young fellow quickly gained their trust, and customers continued to leave money in her jar, enabling her to pay him. Having help allowed more time for Ada to fulfill her duties to Jeremiah as a wife . . . and future mother. She'd recently found out she was three months pregnant.

Renovating Nellie and John's house had

been a labor of love with a dose of bittersweetness thrown into the mix. In the end, they had customized the home to represent themselves, but Jeremiah had chosen to keep some memorabilia that allowed him to feel close to Nellie and John. His parents had visited for the wedding and even stayed in their extra bedroom. There were tears occasionally during their visit, but his mother said God had a way of taking things full circle. Ada's parents had also been at the wedding, which made the day even more perfect for Ada.

Ollie had settled into a life of options. Sometimes, he went to work with Ada. Other days, he stayed with Jeremiah out in the workshop where Jeremiah had continued with his uncle's business. John's clients were happy and pleased that Jeremiah had continued in his uncle's footsteps, and Jeremiah felt good about the decision.

Sometimes, Ada found herself looking at Ollie and thinking about how differently things might have turned out. And while John and Nellie would always be missed and the tragedy of their short lives never forgotten, Ada and Jeremiah believed they were looking down from heaven with smiles on their faces.

Sometimes God created miracles out of

tragedy. Ollie was a miracle in ways that Ada would never understand.

But are we really expected to understand everything God does in our lives, or is it just best to know that He is always working for our good?

A NOTE FROM THE AUTHOR

Decades ago, I was a newspaper reporter when I was one of the first people on the scene of a fatal crash. The driver had apparently fallen asleep, veered off the highway, and collided into a ravine. The car exploded upon impact, killing the female driver and her passenger.

The first responders found a woman's purse in the wreckage, and a little while later, a man showed up at the scene. He said he had circled back when he realized his family members were no longer following him. I stood nearby and watched as the police asked him if the purse in their hands belonged to one of the victims. He nodded, tears streaming down his face.

That was the last time I reported on an accident. I told my editor that I just couldn't do it anymore. I cried throughout the entire ordeal, and maybe I should have been seasoned after covering many car accidents that had left me in tears, but this was the heavy straw that broke my back. So, from then on, I stayed away from anything worse than a fender-bender.

A few weeks later, I received a call from a man who asked if I would come and visit him at his home. He was a retired veterinarian and said he had a story that I might be interested in covering. It sounded far-fetched. The nice man on the other end of the phone said a wounded dog had showed up on his porch wearing a collar with a phone number. When he called to let the owners know that he had found their dog, he was shocked to learn that the dog lived in California and had belonged to the two women who had perished in the aforementioned car accident.

Surely, he was mistaken. I was on the scene as events unfolded. In my mind, no one could have lived through that type of tragedy, especially not a small dog.

But the man was right.

It took a little investigative work for him to find the relatives of the deceased, but he was successful. He told me that the next of kin would be traveling from California to Texas to pick up the dog that very week. I was choking back tears before he had even finished talking to me on the phone. How could this be? What were the chances that a small dog could have survived the impact, crossed four busy lanes of a freeway, and somehow made its way to the doorstep of a retired veterinarian who had nursed him back to health? I accepted his invitation to be at his home when the victims' relatives arrived to pick up the dog.

I covered this story a long time ago. Though I'm a huge dog lover, I don't remember the breed of dog; he wasn't a big dog and was super friendly. I can still envision the man's living room where we gathered, and it will forever be etched in my memories when the relatives of the deceased walked into the room, saw the dog, and cried along with me and the kind man who had saved the animal.

I used this experience as an inspiration to create this fictionalized story of *An Amish Healing.* That reunion was the catalyst, as the scene between the relatives and the dog will stay with me forever.

Whether in real life or through fiction, God does work in mysterious ways. He doesn't cause the bad things, but He can turn a tragedy into a time of hope during an unimaginable loss.

In my own life, I am a pet owner with two large dogs. They can't wear collars, so they are microchipped. In the real story, the dog had a collar, but collars can get lost or are unsuitable for some breeds. Consider having your beloved pet chipped so they can find their way back to you in the event of an emergency.

In summary, I believe in miracles. The big ones, the little ones . . . and even those involving our furry friends and the lives they touch.

Be blessed. Watch for miracles.
Love, Beth

READING GROUP GUIDE FOR AN AMISH HEALING

1. Since this story is based on a real-life experience, how do you think the dog actually survived? Luck? A miracle? Some other explanation?

2. Ada and Jeremiah are both drawn to each other the first time they are introduced, despite the unfortunate circumstances that surround them. Is physical attraction enough to foster true love as they get to know each other? Or, does a person's true character shine from within and reveal more about a person than just their outward appearance?

3. How did you feel about Jeremiah choosing to live in Nellie and John's house? Would you have made that same choice given the situation?

4. Sisters Lizzie and Esther are popular characters from *The Amish Inn* series. Did you enjoy their reappearance and reading about their shenanigans in this book?

5. There's a good chance that you are an animal lover if you chose this book to read. Or, perhaps you just enjoy Amish stories. What is it about the cover that drew you in? The dog? The Amish woman? Something else?

6. If you could change any part of this story, what would it be and why?

AMISH RECIPES

Ada's Walnut Horn Cookies

Ingredients:
1 1/4 cup all-purpose flour
1/2 cup powdered sugar
2/3 cup ground walnuts
1 teaspoon vanilla extract
1 stick butter (unsalted)
2 tablespoons vanilla sugar
4 tablespoons powdered sugar

Instructions:
> In a large mixing bowl combine sifted flour, sifted powdered sugar and ground walnuts. Add vanilla extract and mix.
> Grate chilled butter and add it to the bowl. Using your hands, combine all the ingredients until you form dough.
> Wrap in plastic wrap or put it into a plastic baggie and chill for 30 minutes in the refrigerator.

> In a small bowl, mix the extra powdered sugar with vanilla sugar and set aside.

> Take a piece of the dough (the size of a small walnut) and roll it into a ball and then into a sausage (about 0.5 inch/1.5 cm in diameter and about 3 inch/8 cm long - cut off any excess if too long).

> Shape the sausage into a crescent and place onto a baking tray lined with baking parchment. Repeat until you have used up all the dough.

> Bake in preheated oven at 400°F for 8-10 minutes.

> The cookies should cool down on the tray before transferring them to a plate and dipping them in powdered sugar.

Ada's Sugar Cream Pie

Ingredients:
1 pie crust (deep dish) at room temperature
4 Tbsp cornstarch
3/4 cup white sugar
4 Tbsp butter melted
2 1/4 cups heavy cream
1 Tbsp vanilla extract

For Topping:
4 Tbsp melted butter
1/4-1/2 cup cinnamon sugar
1/4 or 1/2 cup sugar with 2-3 teaspoons ground cinnamon mixed in.

Instructions:
> Preheat oven to 325 degrees F. Place the pie crust onto a baking sheet. Or, if using a refrigerated crust, lightly grease a 9" pie pan, put the crust in, and set the pan on a baking sheet. Bake for 10-12 minutes or until partially baked. Set aside.

> In a small bowl, mix together the cornstarch and sugar until blended. In a medium saucepan, bring the cornstarch-sugar mixture, melted butter and heavy cream together over medium heat, stirring constantly. When the mixture is thick and creamy, stir in the vanilla.

> Pour the mixture into the pie crust. Drizzle on the melted butter and sprinkle on the cinnamon sugar. Bake for about 25 minutes, then broil for approximately 1 minute. Remove from oven. The pie should be at room temperature before refrigerating for at least one hour to set. Store in fridge.

Ada's Snickerdoodle Cookies

Ingredients:
3 cups all-purpose flour
2 teaspoons cream of tartar
1 teaspoon baking soda
1 and 1/2 teaspoons ground cinnamon
1/2 teaspoon salt
1 cup unsalted butter, softened
1 and 1/3 cup granulated sugar
1 large egg, plus 1 large egg yolk, at room temperature
2 teaspoons vanilla extract

For Topping:
1/3 cup granulated sugar
1 teaspoon ground cinnamon

Instructions:
> Preheat oven to 375°F. Line two large cookie sheets with parchment paper.

> Make the topping: Combine the granulated sugar and cinnamon together in a small bowl.

> Make the cookies: Whisk the flour, cream of tartar, baking soda, cinnamon, and salt together in a medium bowl.

> In a large bowl, beat the butter and granulated sugar together on high speed until smooth and creamy, 2-3 minutes. Add

the egg, egg yolk, and vanilla extract. Beat on medium-high speed until combined. Switch to low speed and slowly add the dry ingredients to the wet ingredients in 3 different parts. The dough should be thick.

> Roll cookie dough into balls — about 1.5 Tablespoons of cookie dough each. Roll the dough balls in cinnamon-sugar topping. Sprinkle extra cinnamon-sugar on top if desired. Arrange 3 inches apart on the baking sheets.

> Bake cookies for 10 minutes. The cookies should be puffy and soft. When they are still warm, lightly press down on them with the back of a spoon or fork to flatten them out. Cookies need to cool on the baking sheet for 10 minutes before transferring to a wire rack to cool completely.

ACKNOWLEDGMENTS

Thank you to my sweet daughter-in-law, Casey Roberts, for gracing the cover of *An Amish Healing*. Over the years, I have watched you grow into a beautiful young woman who has faced challenges head-on with strength and perseverance — knowing that all things are possible through Christ who strengthens us . . . always.

To my editors (and dear friends for life) Audrey Wick and Janet Murphy, you gals rock. I couldn't continue to travel along this path without your keen insight and attention to detail. Thank you for everything. I love you both.

I'm fortunate to have an amazing street team — *Wiseman's Warriors* — as they named themselves. Many of you have been with me from the beginning, and my gratefulness goes beyond just words. You are a wonderful group of ladies, and I deeply appreciate all you do to promote my books.

My family and friends continue to support me in this sometimes crazy world of publishing, which ebbs and flows. I'm blessed to have so many wonderful people in my life. Special thanks to my husband, Patrick, who continues to encourage me to follow my dreams. I love you, Dear.

And, as always, my ultimate thanks go to my Heavenly Father, who blesses me with stories to tell that I hope will continue to glorify Him and touch the lives of my readers.

■ ■ ■ ■

Ollie's Story:
An Amish Healing
Redux
A Short Story

■ ■ ■ ■

*To my beloved fur babies —
Rocky and Adrian*

GLOSSARY

ach: oh
boppli: baby
daed: dad
danki: thank you
Englisch/Englischer: non-Amish person
Gott: God
gut nacho: good night
haus: house
lieb/liebed: love/loved
mei: my
nee: no
sohn: son
wie bischt: hello/how are you?
ya: yes

CHAPTER 1

Where are my humans? And why do my paws, snout, and belly hurt?

Hank instinctively carried himself away from the biggest fire he'd ever seen in his short life. Orange glowing flames shot to the sky amid a billowing cloud of black smoke. It smelled like the gas Mr. Hoover had put in the car earlier — the vehicle that was taking them home to Montgomery, Indiana. They were returning from a vacation in Pennsylvania to visit Nellie and John's family.

Where are Nellie and John? They would know how to help Hank. They were the most loving pet owners alive. Even though he'd never lived with anyone else, Hank was sure of it.

As ice crunched beneath muddy paws that ached, Hank's belly hurt, but not the same crampy way as when he was hungry. This was different. In addition to the pain in his stomach, there was a burning sensation on his snout, and when he licked his parched lips, he tasted what he thought was blood.

Loud sirens were everywhere, with flashing blue and red lights and people rushing around all over the place. He'd never seen anything like this, and again, he wondered where Nellie and John were.

He huddled beneath a small tree at the far end of the ravine, away from the crowd, eying what used to be the car they'd traveled in. He shuddered as boom after boom lit up the sky, sending debris flying in all directions.

As he thought back, he recalled Nellie screaming, a loud and scary sound. Hank had closed his eyes from within the small carrier he'd been traveling in. He loved the enclosure filled with blankets and his favorite toys. He remembered a strange feeling, almost as if the vehicle was flying. It was only his second time to travel in a car. Normally, he rode with Nellie and John in a black buggy that was pulled by one of their horses.

His mind blurred, and even at his young age — ten months, he thought — he'd sensed impending doom. The pungent smells, the flying, the screaming . . .

Then, before he'd been able to grasp what

was happening, it felt as if he was transported on a feathery cloud that landed him beneath the tree where he now sat, shivering and in pain.

As he tried to ignore the smoke, the fire, and the chaos, he forced himself to stand, flinching from the pain. His eyes scanned the people who were gathering around the ravine where the smoke was still heavy, but the fire was becoming smaller. Cars had pulled over along the two-lane highway. Women had their mouths covered with their hands. Most of the men shook their heads with drawn expressions on their faces. Some of them wore straw hats like the people Hank was used to being around. Others were in clothes that Nellie said the *Englishers* wore, bright colors and different styles. But almost everyone had on a coat, and as small icy pellets pounded against Hank's fur, he knew he had to find his way home. He'd heard John tell Nellie that they were close to home.

He'd also heard the man driving — Charles — say there was ice on the roads so he would have to slow down.

Hank began shivering so badly from the cold and the pain that was getting worse that he wanted to just lie down in the snow. But something inside nudged him to be strong. Nellie and John would want him to find his way home.

Trembling, he began his trek, on shaky legs, in the direction he thought would take him to his house. He thought his home was on the other side of the highway, and he had no idea how to cross the roadway without getting run over. But it was his only way to get home. Nellie and John would find a way to meet him there, then everything would be okay. Nellie would doctor him the way she had done when he'd stepped on a nail in the barn. It had hurt a lot and caused his foot to swell, and he had to eat pills mashed up in his food for a while. None of it had been pleasant, but Nellie's sweet voice and gentle care had left him knowing he would be okay.

Hank forced himself to walk. Each step felt like he was walking on pins and needles, the kind found in Nellie's sewing basket. He felt ice accumulating on his ears, and the blood on his nose felt like it was freezing.

He eyed the two-lane highway. Home was on the other side. It had to be.

When he'd finally inched closer to the roadway, cars flew by, splashing a wintry mix of ice and snow in his direction. He shook all over. A few of the automobiles, as he'd heard Nellie call the cars, slowed and stopped. Some people stepped out of them while others peered out their windows.

Hank knew that if he didn't try to run across the highway now, he might not ever be able to get to the other side where home was.

His paws ached as he made his way in front of a car that might have been green. He'd heard Nellie and John talk about colors, but he didn't think he saw the same colors as his owners.

The big dark-colored car slammed on the brakes, which reminded Hank of the way their driver must have hit the brakes before all the bad stuff happened. Hank braced for impact by instinctively laying on his belly even though the pain stabbed at his abdomen like a knife. He opened his eyes in time to see four wheels, two on each side, zoom by, delivering a whoosh of icy snow that filled his nostrils, making it hard for him to breathe.

He forced himself to stand on all four paws, searing pain in every step as he weaved his way through the traffic. Thoughts of a warm fire, Nellie's gentle touch, and his special spot on the recliner in the living room were all that kept him going.

Hank had the best owners, and they'd get

**him all fixed up.
He just had to find his way home.**

Chapter 2

Over the next few dizzying hours, time crawled slowly. Hank's paws ached, and his throat was so dry he found himself panting uncontrollably.

After crossing the highway, he was in the middle of a field, the kind of land where John turned grass into food for the cows to eat. Hank liked to lay on the back of the couch by the window and watch John guide the mules as he chopped the grass up and then rolled it into big bales. On pretty days, he loved to roll around in the freshly cut hay.

But the grass in this field was tall and icy, pricking Hank's paws and sides with each painful step. As his vision began to blur from the snow, he thought about giving up. There wasn't even any blood coming from his nose. It felt frozen in place, and Hank feared that Nellie and John might never find him out here in the overgrown field, frozen to death.

He laid down–panting, sore, and defeated–before he closed his eyes to succumb to whatever was happening. But a loud voice in the icy wind bellowed for him to take a deep breath.

Maybe he'd dreamed it, but Hank lifted his head, sniffed the air, and smelled smoke. As he struggled to take breaths around the frozen blood on his nose and mouth, he recognized the welcoming aroma. It wasn't like the stinky smoke at the ravine. It was the woody smell of Nellie and John's fireplace, which meant he was close to home.

Just a little bit farther, he thought as he struggled to stand.

Hank wasn't sure if he could take one more step, but the feathery feel of something beneath his paws warmed not only the pads of his feet but his resolve. He had to make it home. Giving up wasn't an option if he wanted to see Nellie and John again, if he wanted the warmth of the fire, Nellie's gentle touch, and the feel of the soft cushion beneath him in his favorite recliner.

As he shuffled across the field, he forced himself to pick up speed, the pain piercing his paws now, but there was a white house in the distance. It wasn't Nellie and John's home. At least, he didn't think so. With everything blanketed in white, it was hard to tell. But a swirling cloud of gray smoke rose from a chimney like the one at Nellie and John's house.

Someone would help him. Hank just had to get there. He limped the final course to the stranger's house, but moved in an awkward, off-balanced pace to get there.

Hank eyed the porch steps covered in slick, icy snow. Four more steps, and he would be underneath the protection of a covered space. Hopefully, whoever lived there would find him and take him in.

He slid twice trying to paw his way up the slippery steps. Finally, he made it, found his way across the porch, and curled up behind a rocking chair. Hank wanted to bark and call for help, but when he tried to utter a sound, only a whimper escaped. He closed his eyes to rest as darkness began to fall.

Hank wasn't sure how long he slept, but when he blinked his eyes open, the sun was shining. Half his body was in the shadow of the rocking chair, and he could feel the heat of the sun on part of his back.

Yawning was painful as he took in his surroundings, still shivering from the cold and unwilling to move. He ached from head to toe. Why hadn't anyone found him?

He ran his tongue along his bottom lip, which seemed to have scabbed from the blood on his snout.

This was a smaller house than John and Nellie's. The porch wasn't as long, and the barn was much closer than at his owners' house. But whoever lived here must be the same kind of people because a black buggy was on the other side of the fenced front yard. The white picket fence was like the one at his home, and there was a cleared stone pathway that led across the yard to the house. On either side, brownish hues of dry grass poked through the melting snow.

Hank longed to make his way down the steps and into the yard. Despite his wounds, he had to "go potty" as Nellie called it. But when he tried to stand up, his paws wouldn't allow it, and a burning sensation on his underside caused him to fold into himself. He was tempted to put a paw across his face when he tinkled in place, but his snout was too sore to hide his shame. He was forced to lay in his own urine, worried that if he was found, no one would help him because he stunk. He couldn't remember when he'd eaten or drunk anything, so maybe he didn't smell as bad as he felt. His throat was dry, and he still didn't feel like he could bark.

He was startled when the screen door on

the porch opened with a squeak. A woman stepped across the threshold carrying a basket and a box, then she closed the wooden door behind her. Hank's ears perked up at the smell of food, but when he tried again to bark, nothing came out. His heart ached when the woman began to move down the porch steps.

She wore a black overcoat and black bonnet, just like Nellie wore during the cold months. But this woman didn't look like Nellie, who had dark hair. This lady had strands of light-colored hair that escaped from her bonnet.

Hank tried to bark again, but only a small whimper escaped. All he could do was dream about the warmth inside the house and about Nellie and John eventually finding him.

Suddenly, the woman looked over her shoulder and backed up until she stood on the porch staring at Hank. Would she help him or shoo him away? He'd heard some people don't like dogs.

She moved slowly, placing her basket and box atop one of the other three rocking chairs on the porch. After she moved toward him, she squatted down a couple of feet away. "*Wie bischt, mei* little friend."

Hank raised his head a little higher even

though his snout screamed in opposition, aching all the while as he stuck out his tongue and panted, partially from fear but more so in anticipation of someone taking care of him.

The woman inched closer to him. *"Wie bischt,"* she repeated barely above a whisper. "Are you going to let me help you?"

Hank's insides warmed at the tenderness in her voice.

She offered Hank the topside of her hand like he'd seen other people do when they were first introduced to a furry friend. Hank sniffed her hand, and while she didn't look like Nellie, she smelled like Nellie. *Maybe lavender soap.*

The woman began to stroke Hank's back, and with each stroke, she drew back dirt and icy mud from his fur. Her actions were soothing, but his belly burned, and when he moved, he saw fresh blood, which caused him to tremble with fear more than pain. Maybe he was going to die after all.

She took back her hand, frowned, and studied him for a long while before she slipped both hands underneath him. *What's she doing?*

As she lifted Hank into her arms, he yelped. He was happy to have his voice back, but he'd caused the woman to jump, which wasn't his intention. Hank didn't want her to drop him or be afraid of him. He lowered his head into the nook of her arm, ashamed that he was getting icy dirt on her black coat, not to mention how he must smell.

The woman — he wished he knew her name — carried him into the house, and a blast of warm air hit him like welcomed sunshine after a bath. She took him straight to the bathroom, wrapped him in a towel, and then cradled him in her arms like humans cradle a baby. Hank felt safe even though he hurt all over.

Wait . . . no, no, no. She was heading back to the porch with him. *Please don't leave me in the cold to die.*

Still holding him, she retrieved her bag and box of whatever smelled so good from the porch and placed them on the kitchen table. Hank breathed a huge sigh of relief when they were back in the warm house.

After crossing through the living room, they entered a small room with a metal exam table. Hank had seen a room like this before, and he began to tremble again. He remembered getting shots and other unpleasantries that had occurred atop a table like this one.

The lady placed a clean white towel on

the table before laying Hank down. The billowy towel began to absorb dirt and blood as his new caretaker began to inspect every inch of him. His trembling stilled. It was warm in the room, but he began to pant, and his breaths were becoming more labored. The woman was gentle with her touch, but Hank wasn't looking forward to being poked and prodded no matter how pretty the lady was, how soft her hands were, or how sweet her voice.

As she eased him onto his side, more blood oozed from his belly. He didn't want her touching that area. She leaned closer to him, her face near his, as she gently scratched the top of his head.

"*Ach, mei* friend, we need to stitch this up." The woman flinched, causing a flurry of anxiety to rush over Hank. *Stitch this up? What does that mean?* "I'm sorry," she said, her face crinkled into an expression that worried Hank even more.

She reached for a bottle from a shelf against the wall, shook the contents into a small shallow bowl, and then offered it to Hank. He moved his head into a position where he could sniff the bowl. It wasn't water, but he began to lap up the liquid. He was so thirsty, and even though it tasted grainy and strange, he drank it all.

"There you go," she said, smiling now, and Hank's throat didn't feel as dry. *That wasn't so bad.* Then she reached for another bottle, cringing again, and Hank's stomach churned. "This will sting a bit."

Sting? He'd heard that word. Nellie had wrangled with a bee, and a sting was the result. It had brought tears to her eyes. *Wait . . . I don't want any stings.* But when the liquid met with his matted wound, Hank gave her a warning in the form of a nip on her arm. It wasn't meant to hurt her, just to let her know that whatever she poured on his belly was causing him pain.

Right away, he felt bad for snapping at her, and he was glad to see he hadn't broken the surface. Even though pain engulfed his tummy, he sensed she was trying to help him. But he wasn't interested in her getting near his belly.

She touched him where it hurt anyway, pressing a warm towel against the place where all the blood was coming from, and then she began to rub some thick and milky stuff all around the area, and it didn't feel good at all. But he didn't have the heart to snap at her again.

After she sprinkled more grainy droplets into a bowl of warm water, she offered it to him, and Hank drank it all. Within seconds, his head began to spin, the room became blurry, and he could feel an odd sensation in his belly. Was she giving him those stitches she'd mentioned?

He wasn't sure. He felt pressure, but it didn't hurt. And he was starting not to care what she did as he began to yawn.

After a while, he felt awake but asleep, an odd feeling he wasn't familiar with, but he wasn't in nearly as much pain.

"There. You look like a new doggie," she said, smiling.

Hank smiled on the inside as the room spun.

"I have to leave you for a while to attend two funerals." Her smile vanished as she retrieved a kennel.

Hank fought the fogginess in his mind as she eased him into the cage. He didn't want to be confined. He wanted to be back in her arms, feeling safe like he did before.

Funerals? Who died? And where are Nellie and John?

CHAPTER 3

When Hank opened his eyes, it took him a few minutes to remember where he was. In a kennel atop the metal table. He felt clean and didn't smell badly anymore, but his belly was tight, tender, and covered with some sort of dressing. He also had something that felt like a bandage across his snout and another one by his left ear. *Gauze.* That's what he'd heard Nellie call it when she doctored John's arm once.

Where was the pretty lady with the soft voice and light-colored hair? He began to whimper, and the louder his whine became, the more his head hurt. How long could he survive in this kennel? Then, he saw a small platter of water in the far corner of what he feared might be his new home.

Laying almost sideways on his belly, in an awkward position to avoid the tenderness on his tummy, he began to drink. He felt a little better with each gulp, but he hoped he didn't sleep again. He needed to be alert and aware of his surroundings.

He wailed even louder between panting when he heard a door open somewhere in the house. Even though he tried to bark, only pitiful moans escaped, but he made as much noise as he could until he heard loud footsteps heading his way. His ears perked up when he saw it was the woman who had taken him in.

"You poor *boppli*." She unlatched the lever on the kennel and slowly reached a hand inside, gently stroking Hank's back, which seemed to be one of the few places where he didn't have a bandage. "I'm sorry I left you," she said.

Hank's panting began to slow down as the feel of the lady's gentle touch calmed him. He wanted to stand, though, so on shaky legs, he lifted himself to his feet.

"Will you let me hold you?" She patted the entrance of the kennel, and Hank shuffled slowly toward her, then he let her ease her arms beneath him. He stifled a yelp since she moved slowly and took care to maneuver around his wounds, eventually cradling him like a baby. Even though he was sore, he felt safe in her arms.

She moved out of the small room with the kennel and shelves and into the big room with the couch. "You're shivering." She laid him down on the couch before she hung her black cape and bonnet on the rack by the front door, and then she wriggled out of her boots.

Hank trembled, partly from the cold, but he was also apprehensive. Nothing was familiar. Where were Nellie and John? He missed his favorite recliner, but staying put on this new furniture didn't require much effort. And when was he going to get some food?

After the woman added a log to the glowing embers in her fireplace, she sat on the couch and eased Hank into her arms.

He closed his eyes. If he were a cat, he'd be purring. He liked being in her arms.

She lowered her face to his, almost touching the bandage on his nose, and Hank decided that she deserved a big wet kiss.

"Danki," she said as she giggled before she began to rock him in her arms. Hank yawned.

"Do you think I'll ever see that man again?" She sighed, still cradling him like a baby. "I'm thinking I won't."

Hank didn't open his eyes, hoping she would keep talking. Maybe she would offer a clue about his owners. *What man? John?*

"If no one claims you, would you like to

stay here?" She leaned down again and lowered her nose to Hank's snout without touching the bandage on his face. Hank attempted to nod, and the woman chuckled. "Then it's settled. And we need a name for you."

She was a nice lady, but . . . *I have a name. Hank. And my owners are John and Nellie.*

His new friend was startled when her phone rang in her purse. Hank shifted slightly as she reached for it on the coffee table.

He'd heard Nellie and others say that phones weren't allowed or were for emergencies. Hank assumed there must be a lot of emergencies because everyone around him had a phone.

The woman listened to the speaker, then laughed and said, "Lizzie . . . the man is grieving, and he lives in another state. I think your matchmaking skills might be put to better use somewhere else."

Hank's ears perked up. *Grieving?* He was pretty sure that was a type of sadness. But it was confusing since his new caregiver had laughed prior to the comment.

"*Nee,* Lizzie, I don't think I should come. We have more snow on the way." Hank's chest tightened as he wondered if he would be left in the kennel again. He lifted his eyes to hers, willing her to see how he felt inside. Could she see how scared he would be if she left him unattended?

She — again he wondered what her name was — listened for a few moments, then said, "I'm sure the family will return to settle Nellie and John's affairs. If it's *Gott's* plan for me to see Jeremiah again, then it will happen."

Jeremiah. That name sounded familiar, but he wasn't sure why. Hank tried to find his voice, to bark, to let this nice lady know that Nellie and John were his owners, but only a whimper escaped. Right away, the woman's hand found his special spot behind his good ear and rubbed. It felt so satisfying, but Hank's thoughts were scrambled like the leftover eggs Nellie fed him sometimes.

Where are Nellie and John? Someone needed to let them know that Hank was safe. And, as nice as this lady was, Hank missed his people, his chair, his home. *And who is Jeremiah?* he wondered again.

The woman listened to the other person talking for a while, then she stiffened all over and stopped rubbing Hank behind his ear.

"What do you mean that someone should have spoken at the funeral about the dog who perished in the accident? I didn't know Nellie and John had a dog." The lady put a hand to her mouth and listened again. "Are you saying that Nellie and John took their dog on vacation to Pennsylvania with them?"

Yes! Yes! They took me with them to Pennsylvania, and we were almost home when we got separated. What accident? Were John and Nellie hurt?

The lady listened some more. Hank held his breath and strained to hear, but he couldn't.

"Did you say the dog was a Border Collie?" She looked down at Hank and blinked her eyes a few times. Her eyes glassed over with moisture.

The call ended, and she put the phone beside her on the couch before she stood up carrying Hank.

Please don't put me back in the kennel. I'm feeling confused. I miss Nellie and John. Hank had so many questions he wished he could verbalize so this woman could help him get home.

But she didn't go toward the room with the kennel. Instead, she pulled back a pretty cover on a big bed in another room and laid him down. After she put on her bedclothes and crawled under the covers, she reached over and rubbed Hank's back. He liked it when she did that, but he couldn't fully appreciate it with all these thoughts swirling around in his mind.

"You can't possibly be Nellie and John's dog." The lady sniffled. "That would be nothing short of a miracle."

Then I guess I'm a miracle. Hank's head hurt. So did his heart. *Please take me to Nellie and John. They must be really worried about me.*

Chapter 4

Ollie wasn't sure how much time had gone by, maybe seven or eight days. *Ollie.* That's what she had started calling him. He found his voice and barked for the first couple of days, hoping she would get the message. His name was Hank.

But Ollie was starting to grow on him, as was this lady. She even bought him a ball to play with outside when the weather was nice enough. He decided he would be Ollie until he was reunited with Nellie and John. Then he'd be back to Hank.

"Come on, Ollie, we need to get ready to go on a short trip." She stood from where she sat in a chair on the front porch, a blanket wrapped around her shoulders.

Ollie hopped through the white slush of melted snow with his new yellow tennis ball in his mouth. He dropped it at her feet just like she'd taught him to do. She leaned down, smiling, and scratched him behind the ears. He was in pretty good shape, he thought, with just a small bandage on his nose. *Where are we going? What kind of trip?* They hadn't left the house since Ollie arrived, and he liked it here. And he liked her. But most nights, when he fell asleep, he thought about Nellie and John.

"We've got to go see Dr. Farley." She scooped him into her arms. "You might have an owner who is missing you."

I do, I do! Nellie and John. Was she taking him to see them?

He wagged his tail the whole time the lady dressed in her black cape and bonnet, then she slipped into her boots and retrieved her purse from the couch. There was a small red travel-sized kennel by the front door. It was almost exactly like the one Nellie and John used to put him in when they carted him around town. He didn't mind. When the buggies hit a rut, it could get bouncy, and he felt safe in the enclosure. *But wait . . .*

Ollie was pretty sure he'd been in a kennel like this when he'd lost track of Nellie and John. He remembered the man driving the car saying he wanted to get some coffee, so they'd stopped. Ollie had been given a snack and done his business. He'd fallen asleep after that.

The next thing he knew, there was fire, he

was hurting, and he couldn't find Nellie and John.

He stopped wagging his tail, his recollections muddled now.

Once they got on the road, there was solace in the sound of the clip-clop of hooves, a familiar sound that lulled him into a tranquil state. But it wasn't long before they stopped in front of a small building. After Ollie was out of the kennel, the lady encircled his neck with a collar, then attached a leash and walked him inside. He'd never worn a collar. It felt foreign but not unpleasant.

She told the woman behind a glass window that she was here to see Dr. Farley, then she sat in one of the chairs in the room. Ollie tucked his tail between his legs from where he sat on the cold floor in front of her as he wondered which one of them needed doctoring.

He wasn't sure how much time had passed, but eventually a woman came from behind a door and waved her arm like she wanted them to follow her. So, they did.

They were led into a room like at the lady's house, but it was bigger. There was a metal table in the center, and there were shelves lined with equipment and bottles. Ollie tensed. He vaguely remembered being in a room like this when he was a puppy. And he was pretty sure there were shots involved. He didn't think he liked this place.

"Ada, Dr. Farley will be in shortly," the woman said, smiling before she left the room and closed the door behind her.

Ollie's ears perked up. *Ada.* Now he had a name for his new friend. *Ada, Ada, Ada,* he repeated over and over in his mind so he wouldn't forget.

But after that news sunk in, he began to shiver, a mixture of the cold temperature in the room and fear of being poked and prodded.

"You're okay, Ollie," Ada said.

Ada, Ada, Ada. He liked her name.

He wanted to believe her, that he was okay, that no harm would come to him — or to Ada.

A white-headed man entered the room, tall and stout, and without any warning whatsoever, he lifted Ollie into his arms and placed him on the cold metal table. He wasn't as gentle as Ada, but he did manage to avoid the tender spot on his belly. "Gloria said we're checking for a microchip today. I don't recognize this animal. If he has a chip, someone else must have inserted it."

"*Ya.*" Ada cleared her throat. "He's a stray that I've had for a week. The weather wasn't *gut,* and he needed stitches. Today is the first day I felt like he was fit for travel."

Ollie wasn't sure if that was true. It seemed like the weather had been pretty good for a couple of days. At least better than it had been. Sunshine peeked through the clouds, lending a crisp breeze that made Ollie's fur fluffy.

"Can you please check him out thoroughly and make sure I didn't miss anything and that the place where I put stitches looks okay?"

Suddenly, Dr. Farley's hands were all over Ollie, and he offered up a low, guttural growl to let the older man know that he wasn't enjoying this. The doctor had to pry open Ollie's mouth to shine a light inside.

"Ada, you've done good work," the man said, still shining a light in Ollie's mouth. "I'm guessing he's around ten or eleven months old based on his size and his teeth."

Finally, Ollie was able to close his mouth. He eyed the distance from the table to the floor and decided that jumping down wasn't an option.

"I didn't think he was very old. He's playful and looks like he hasn't grown into his paws yet." Her voice sounded shaky as she spoke, then she dabbed at her eyes with a handkerchief she had in the pocket of her cape.

Dr. Farley had one hand on Ollie, as if to keep him from jumping down. Even though he'd decided against that, he wanted to be near Ada. Something was wrong with her. He could feel her sadness.

"Oh, dear. It looks like someone has gotten attached." The doctor began to stroke Ollie's back, and he wasn't sure if that motion was a trick or genuine. He remembered getting poked with a long needle once when a stranger stroked his back while he was atop a metal table.

"I guess I have gotten attached. But if he has owners who are missing him, then he should be returned." Ada swiped at her eyes with the tissue again.

Yes! Yes! I have owners. And I'm sure John and Nellie miss me!

"Well, let's have a look." The doctor took a step backward and picked up a round instrument, and Ollie held his breath and braced for whatever was coming, emitting a low growl since he was unsure. But the man only moved the round instrument all around Ollie's body — his neck, his back, and even down his legs.

Suddenly, there was a beep. Ada gasped before she covered her mouth with her hand, and her eyes got all wet.

"I need Gloria to run this registration number," Dr. Farley said. "I'll be back in a few minutes with the information."

After the door closed, Ada wrapped her arms around Ollie and took him off the table, putting him in her lap. She held him close and rubbed noses with him. A tear rolled down her cheek, and it made Ollie's heart hurt. He licked it away. *Why are you crying?*

"You'll be going home to your owners soon," she said.

Ollie's tail went into a full wag. *Nellie and John?* But then he looked up at Ada as another tear rolled down her cheek. *Will I ever see her again?* That thought didn't make him feel very good.

"I wonder what your real name is," she said barely above a whisper.

It's Hank. But he wouldn't mind if she kept calling him Ollie if it would keep her from crying. He ran his tongue across her face, the same way he'd been doing every morning when he felt it was time for her to wake up. He'd been sleeping in her bed all week. But now, he just wanted to comfort her.

The gray-headed man — Dr. Farley — walked into the room a few moments later, his face ashen, his jowls drooping. He locked eyes with Ada. "This animal is registered to Nellie and John Troyer. It's odd that the name of the dog isn't included in the information, but he is registered to the Troyers."

Yes! Yes! They are my owners! Ollie wagged his tail. Soon, he'd be home. He glanced at Ada, who sniffled. Something tugged at his heart from deep inside.

Dr. Farley scratched his cheek as he shook his head. "I saw the article about the fatal accident in the local newspaper. Such a terrible thing to happen, especially so close to home." Sighing, he leaned against the counter and stuffed his hands in the pockets of his crisp white doctor's coat. "I remember reading that they didn't have any family who lived nearby."

Wait, wait, wait. What does 'fatal' mean?

Ada held Ollie a little closer. She smelled good, and he liked being with her, but he was confused about Nellie and John.

"I met Nellie and John's family while they were here for the funeral." She glanced at Ollie. "Nellie and John had taken Ollie — or whatever his real name is — with them to Pennsylvania. He was in the car during their commute home when the car exploded in the ravine." She squeezed Ollie even closer. "He couldn't have survived." She blinked her eyes as she lifted her head to Dr. Farley's gaze. "This can't be the same dog."

Ollie listened, but he was having some strange flashbacks about what might have happened. *Screaming . . . the fire . . .* Had he flown in his kennel through the air?

The older man in the white coat said, "I had Gloria run the information twice on the scanner just to be sure. Maybe he was ejected out of the car before it . . . um, exploded."

Ada lowered her head, holding Ollie so tight he could barely breathe, but he didn't wiggle out of her embrace. She seemed to need him. "The right thing to do is to contact the extended family. Maybe they want him," Ada said, her voice still shaky.

"Do you have a way to reach them?" Dr. Farley leaned against the counter and folded his arms across his chest.

"*Ya.* They stayed at The Peony Inn. I'm sure Lizzie and Esther, the owners, have contact information."

"I know this is difficult, and I will pray for you, Ada."

After the doctor excused himself, citing other patients he needed to see, Ada put Ollie on the floor, secured his leash to his collar, and they left the building and headed toward her covered buggy.

She got him settled in the red carrier on the seat beside her, then she lowered her head into her hands and cried.

Ollie trembled all over. Ada was sad. And, if he'd heard and understood correctly, Nellie and John had crossed over their version of the rainbow bridge.

Are they gone forever?

Ollie's heart hurt in an unfamiliar way.

He glanced at Ada, who was still sobbing. He wanted out of the kennel. As much as he hurt, he wanted to comfort Ada. Apparently, she was in pain, too, and that tugged at his heart as much as the reality that he wouldn't see Nellie and John again.

Dogs don't cry the same way humans do, but Ollie was crying on the inside.

CHAPTER 5

They didn't go to Ada's home or to Ollie's. Instead, they went to a big house called The Peony Inn. Two nice older ladies named Esther and Lizzie ushered them into the living room. After the women consoled Ada, it was decided that they needed to make a phone call to a man named Jeremiah. The name was still familiar to Ollie, but he wasn't sure why.

Ada held Ollie in her lap, too tightly, but he allowed it as he tried to familiarize himself with this new place. He sniffed the air and liked the smells here. Cedar from the fireplace hung in the air with a background aroma of something yummy cooking in the oven.

The smaller of the two women punched buttons on the phone, then laid it down on the coffee table before she began to speak. "I know this might be hard to believe, but apparently John and Nellie's dog survived. I can't recall his name, but I know it's their dog because I saw him at their *haus.*" The woman paused and drew in a deep breath before she went on. "It's a miracle, really."

That was the second time Ollie had heard the word 'miracle'.

The ladies huddled around the phone, and even though Ollie didn't understand exactly what was said, he'd gathered two things from the conversation. Nellie and John were not coming back for him. And a man named Jeremiah was coming to pick him up, presumably to take Ollie back to the place where he had vacationed with Nellie and John.

He recalled the house and the people they visited. They'd been nice. But there was a grouchy dog where they had vacationed. *Buster.* Ollie clenched his jaw as he recalled Buster's dislike of him, the way the big animal had bared his teeth and let it be known that Ollie was in his territory. *Is that where I'm going next?* He shivered at the possibility.

Ollie tuned out the rest of the conversation, mostly because he didn't understand it, and he'd gathered the information he needed as it pertained to him and his future. A future that didn't look bright.

As Ada continued to coddle him, Ollie

decided that if he couldn't be with Nellie and John, he wanted to stay with her. Now, he wondered if that was even an option.

His insides began to settle after they'd left the big home and the two older women. A warm feeling washed over him when they arrived back at Ada's house after she'd offered him extra treats. Maybe she had sensed his anxiety. These weren't like regular treats from a box. Ada cooked treats for Ollie, and they tasted like peanut butter. He calmed down even more when they finally went to bed that evening. Ollie inched closer to her until she put her hand atop his head, then scratched behind his ears. "You're a *gut* boy, Ollie."

As good as her reassuring words and touch felt, his heart hurt for Nellie and John, and he worried about having to leave Ada to go away with the man named Jeremiah.

Ollie wasn't sleepy, and little by little, details were swimming into his mind filled with turbulence and heartbreak. *Nellie and John are gone.*

As Ada continued to stroke Ollie's back, he wondered if humans knew that dogs cried, even if only on the inside. And Ollie was sobbing buckets.

■ ■ ■ ■

Several weeks passed before Jeremiah showed up at Ada's house one morning with a suitcase at his side. Ollie recognized him as one of the men they'd visited in Pennsylvania, donning a straw hat like their people wore. Now, he was here to pick up Ollie and take him to a faraway home that had only served as a vacation spot. A vacation spot that had housed a large dog that didn't care for Ollie at all. Ollie had tried to make friends, but the family pet, Buster, had no interest in forming a relationship. Just the opposite, Buster wanted Ollie gone.

Ada's house felt like home now, and Ollie had no plans to leave.

Ada held Ollie in her arms as she opened the front door. Even though Ollie recognized the man — Jeremiah — he didn't know him at all. He hadn't spent much time with him while he was in Pennsylvania with Nellie and John. Jeremiah came and went as if he had another house somewhere. This man was a stranger.

"This is unbelievable." Jeremiah shook his head as he gazed at Ollie. "I don't know how to thank you for tending to Hank."

My name is Ollie now.

"Finding out that he was alive was the happiest I've seen *mei mamm* since Nellie and John died," Jeremiah said.

Ollie wondered who Jeremiah's mother was.

"I heard Lavina had liked this cute fellow." Ada leaned down and almost touched her nose to his snout, always careful of the small bandage that remained. Ollie loved it when she did that.

Lavina. He remembered her from their vacation. She was the mom of the family. A nice lady, but so was Ada, and Ollie didn't want to be relocated. He thought about Buster again and shivered.

"And you're welcome. I enjoyed taking care of him." She scratched Ollie behind his good ear as she continued to cradle him in one arm. "I have some medications I'd like to send with you. There are a few places that you still need to keep an eye on, and one spot on his nose that I've been trying to keep covered. Although he isn't fond of the bandage."

Because it itches.

Jeremiah followed her to the room with the metal table and the kennel. Ollie tensed when Ada gently set him on the cold table. "These are the spots I've been keeping a close eye on for infection, but so far, so *gut.*" She took a deep breath and blew it out slowly. "And he loves to play fetch. I'll send the tennis ball that I bought for him with you."

No. I'm not going.

"*Ya,* great. I'll make sure he gets some play time and exercise while I'm here working on the *haus.* It needs some work before we can put it on the market for sale."

Here working on what house? Ollie assumed Jeremiah was taking him back to live with his family in Pennsylvania.

Ada began putting ointments and bandages in a bag.

Jeremiah picked up Ollie with no warning, his hand pressing across the sore spot on his belly. Ollie wanted to snap off his hand, but instead, he growled. Loudly.

"Uh oh," Jeremiah said.

And that was just a warning, Buddy.

Ada reached for Ollie, and his anxiety stilled in the comfort of her arms. "You can't hold him that way," she said rather loudly. "He is still tender right here." She maneuvered Ollie until the remnants of the healing wound on his underbelly were visible, still red with tufts of brown hair growing back and tiny holes where stitches had been. "I'm sorry if I sound snappy. I should have been more clear when I was explaining and showing you his injuries."

Or Jeremiah could have paid better attention. Ollie had seen the way Jeremiah looked at Ada the entire time she was trying to educate him. He'd been more interested in her as opposed to gathering a good understanding of Ollie's medical care.

Ada turned and left the room with Ollie against her chest and his paws propped up on her shoulder. Jeremiah followed. Ollie did his best to bare his teeth at the man as they walked. But it was a bit jarring when Ada thrust Ollie right into Jeremiah's arms when they got to the front door.

"Best of luck to you, and again . . . *mei* sympathies to you and your family." She gazed into Ollie's eyes. "Goodbye, Ollie . . . I mean, Hank."

But I'm Ollie now, remember?

Jeremiah eased backward over the threshold with a tight grip on Ollie. Ada closed the door.

What? Just like that? She's gone?

Ollie was too stunned to move as Jeremiah placed him on the ground, then attached a leash to his collar before picking up a piece of luggage he'd left on the porch, along with another small red suitcase that Ada had filled with medications and bandages. He began to lead Ollie away from Ada's house.

Where was his buggy? Where was a car with a driver in it? *Are we going to walk? How far?* He looked over his shoulder. Ada was inside the house, staring out the window and touching her eyes with a tissue.

Don't let me go, Ada.

Ollie pulled against the leash and dug his heels into the snowy mush, wishing there was a way to fling some right into Jeremiah's face. But he barked instead, as loud as he could. And finally, Ada burst out the door and sprinted down the steps.

"Wait!" she yelled, and Ollie stopped barking and straining against the leash. "Didn't you arrange transportation?" she asked, breathless.

Ollie's hopes fell. He'd thought for sure Ada was coming to take him back inside, that they'd cuddle up in her bed, and that he'd lick her face the next morning when it was time to get up. But he wasn't sure of anything anymore. He jerked the weight of his body until the leash broke free from Jeremiah's hand, then he ran to Ada. Losing Nellie and John had been awful. Ollie wasn't ready to lose Ada too.

"You silly boy," Ada said with her arms stretched wide to intercept him. She enclosed him in the safety of her arms, and he breathed in the smell of her, a mixture of lavender soap, cookies, and bread fresh from the oven. All aromas that Ollie loved, almost as much as he loved Ada. *Don't make me go.*

"Hank is attached to you," Jeremiah said. "I'm not surprised."

Ollie jerked his head around in time to see Jeremiah giving Ada that strange look again, almost like he was lovesick. John used to look at Nellie like that. But this man didn't even know Ada, did he? Ollie barked.

Ada stood up holding Ollie, and once again, for the time being, he felt safe. "He answers to Ollie now." She raised her chin and hugged Ollie closer.

Finally, she set him straight.

"Uh . . ." Jeremiah scratched his cheek, then tipped back the rim of his black hat. "Okay."

"I mean, I didn't know his name, so I just began calling him Ollie, and I think he's used to that." She sighed. "But he's your dog now, so I suppose you can call him whatever you'd like."

What is happening?

Ollie had heard Nellie say once that she was on an emotional roller coaster. It had something to do with an argument with a friend. Ollie hadn't understood exactly what she meant until now. He wasn't sure what a roller coaster was, but he knew his emotions were all over the place.

Ollie twisted in Ada's arms to where he could keep an eye on Jeremiah, but Jeremiah only seemed to have eyes for Ada.

"I like the name Ollie." Jeremiah shrugged, smiling. "And I don't think it matters what we call hm. He clearly adores you."

Yes, so go home now. He turned and licked Ada on the cheek as a thank you.

She chuckled as she pressed her nose to Ollie's. "I've had him for a while." When she finished loving on Ollie, much too soon, she said, "You can't walk all the way to Nellie and John's *haus* balancing a dog on your hip or pulling him along on his leash while toting luggage."

Ollie's heart leapt. *Nellie and John's house?* Had he been wrong this entire time? Were Nellie and John at home waiting for his return? Soon, would he be back in his favorite chair?

"I-I can take you in *mei* buggy to Nellie and John's *haus* if you'd like."

Ollie's heart pounded against his chest. He didn't completely understand what was happening, but he was going home. And Ada was coming with him. He smiled on the inside, verging on happy tears as he swished his tail back and forth with absolute approval.

CHAPTER 6

Jeremiah drove Ada's buggy, and Ollie got to ride in the front seat with Ada holding him. Ada had a bag of Ollie's favorite homemade treats, and she generously gave one to Ollie every time he looked up at her. He was fairly certain she could read his mind.

No one said much, and during the ride, Ada had slipped on a pair of dark sunglasses to cut the glare from the daytime sun, Ollie supposed. Or maybe she didn't want anyone to see her eyes. Nellie used to say that the eyes were the windows to the soul. Maybe she didn't want anyone to see her soul or how she was really feeling. She trembled ever so slightly. Jeremiah probably didn't notice, but Ollie did. He gave her a couple of big wet kisses which brought on a smile each time.

When they arrived at Nellie and John's house, a sense of familiarity filled Ollie with hope. But the yard was untended. John always cleared a neat path in the snow up to the porch, and there was never any of the white stuff on the porch. Today, there was no clear path, and a sludgy white and brown mess was half-melted on the porch.

No one got out of the buggy, and Ollie began to squirm, partly because he was anxious, but he also needed to do his business.

There was a long silence. Ollie wasn't sure what to think. But he wiggled in Ada's arms, hoping she'd get the message.

"Would you like for me to come in with you?" Ada finally asked.

Yes. Ollie was sure Nellie and John would be glad to see Ada too.

"I-I've already put you through enough." Jeremiah smiled, but it didn't look like a real smile to Ollie. He stepped out of the buggy and pulled his suitcases from the backseat. By the time he walked around to the other side of the buggy, Ada had already stepped out and set Ollie on the ground, grasping his leash as she shuffled to a dry patch of grass amid the driveway gravel, where Ollie was finally able to take care of business.

Afterward, Ada turned to Jeremiah and removed her sunglasses. Her eyes were red and moist. "I'll go in with you," she said with a tremor in her voice.

Even though his heart hurt for Ada, he couldn't wait to see John and Nellie, and he had a newfound bounce in his step as they crossed the yard and made their way up the porch steps.

Ada stepped to the side when they reached the front door. Jeremiah set down the suitcases, then fumbled in a side pocket of his jacket until he pulled out a key and unlocked the front door.

Ollie wagged his tail and panted with excitement. *I'm home.*

But it didn't feel like home as he crossed the threshold into the living room. He raised his snout and sniffed the air, then crinkled his nose. It didn't smell like home either. Nellie always had something baking in the oven, yummy aromas like at Ada's house. This house smelled stale, like the leftover smells from a fire.

Ada unhooked Ollie's leash from his collar before she said, "I'll start opening some windows to clear this stale air."

Jeremiah nodded as he took the grate from the fireplace and set it on the wood floor. Someone must have left the old wood and ashes, which caused the house to become stinky. That didn't sound like something

Nellie or John would do.

Ollie stared at his chair, the one he slept in or sat on John's lap when he was home. He began to bark, assuming Nellie and John would have greeted him when he arrived. But as he ran from room to room downstairs, then jogged upstairs, it became clear that no one was home. In addition to the musty air, plumes of dust met with sunrays that shown through hazy windows in every room, dancing in circles around Ollie. He stood still in Nellie and John's bedroom. There weren't any sheets on the bed, and where was the pretty pastel quilt that covered the bed? Ollie eyed the far-left corner at the foot of the bed where he used to sleep.

There was no life in this room. As he rechecked the other upstairs rooms, then the downstairs, the realization hit that his first thoughts had been correct. Nellie and John had left him for good.

Ollie still had one place to check. He ran to the kitchen, but instead of Nellie or John, he found Ada moving things around and tossing items in the trashcan. Ollie walked to his food and water bowls, both with his name from his past life etched into the plastic. A life not so long ago that seemed to collide with whatever was going on now.

He stared at the name on both bowls. *Hank.* But Hank wasn't Hank without Nellie and John.

He glanced up at Ada and wished she could read his mind.

"I know you must be hungry," she said as she reached down and scratched him behind the ears. "And you're being so patient, but I haven't found any dog food yet."

Ollie wasn't hungry. He was confused and scared. Would he be left in this house that now felt like a shell of his former home — a house that smelled bad and with a man he didn't know?

He followed Ada to the living room. Jeremiah had started a new fire, and it smelled more normal to Ollie, but sadness overtook him, and he retreated to the recliner, which used to be his favorite spot in the house. He wasn't sure anymore.

Ollie listened to Ada and Jeremiah talking, and he picked up as much as he could. Nellie and John had died, and Ada would be leaving soon. Ollie would be left here with Jeremiah with nothing familiar but the house and furniture, which didn't compare to the warmth of human companionship from those he knew and trusted.

When Ada picked up her purse, Ollie began to weep on the inside again. *Please don't leave me.*

She was almost to the door when she looked over her shoulder twice at Ollie, locking eyes with him the second time. Her bottom lip trembled, and Ollie didn't want to look away from her, but when he did, he saw that Jeremiah was staring at her while rubbing his chin. Was it hard for Ada to leave Ollie too? Was Jeremiah picking up on that?

The stranger in Ollie's house yawned. "I'm exhausted. I believe the *Englisch* call it jet lag. And since we didn't find any food for Ollie, maybe you could keep him tonight?" He raised an eyebrow.

Ollie straightened as his ears perked up. *Say yes.* As much as he loved this house, it wasn't a home without Nellie and John. And he knew Ada cared about him.

He held his breath and waited. When Ada called his name and squatted down, he ran into her arms, the safest place he knew in the world these days.

Ada and Jeremiah talked, something about going to the store the following day, which caused his stomach to clench until he heard that he would be able to go with them. Right now, he didn't want to be far from Ada, and he was unsure what he would do if anything happened to her as well.

When they got back to Ada's house, they both ate. She doctored Ollie's nose, and after she had showered, they crawled into bed just like they'd been doing for over a month. Ollie didn't want to go back to Nellie and John's house without them there. This was his new home now, and with that thought, he fell asleep quickly, but he still thought about Nellie and John before he dozed off.

The next morning, Ada put Ollie in the portable red kennel in the backseat of her covered buggy. He would rather be on her lap, but he recalled the conversation between Ada and Jeremiah the day before. They were going to pick up Jeremiah and go to the store.

Jeremiah was waiting on the front porch of what used to be Ollie's home when Ada pulled in. He climbed into the passenger side, meaning there was no chance Ollie could ride in Ada's lap. But, from his kennel, he could see out the side window of the buggy. They passed farms and other buggies, and a few cars blew past them. Cars had always scared Ollie. Even more so now. They were big and fast. He cringed every time when they passed in the other lane, and he closed his eyes when a car sped from behind the buggy and went around them.

Ada and Jeremiah talked a lot. Ada even laughed a few times. It seemed like they were becoming friends. Or maybe more than friends. Ollie wasn't sure how he felt about that yet.

Finally, they arrived at the store, and while Ada bundled her cape more tightly around her waist, Jeremiah tethered the horse, then reached into the kennel and picked up Ollie. He yelped. The man didn't know how to hold him without hitting the sore spot on his belly, and he wanted Ada to carry him.

"Uh, oh." Jeremiah frowned. "Did I do something to hurt him or pick him up wrong again? Maybe he's not completely healed?"

Ollie seethed on the inside, stifling a grumble. He'd been shown how to hold Ollie before. Didn't he listen?

"He might still be sore, but he should be fine." Ada reached out her arms, and Ollie wasted no time wiggling out of Jeremiah's hold on him.

"He's attached to you," Jeremiah said again.

Yes. Ollie snuggled into Ada's arms.

"Maybe," she said. "I've had him for a while. And, surprisingly, no one has brought any other animals for me to tend to, so *mei* attention has been solely on him."

As it should be. He licked her on the face, and she smiled.

Ollie had only been around one other dog, and it had been while he was vacationing with Nellie and John — that big dog, Buster, who liked to show off his sharp teeth.

Inside the store, Jeremiah and Ada were talking to two ladies dressed the same way as Ada. Ollie took the opportunity to look around from his perch inside a metal shopping cart. There were all kinds of things to see. Food, clothes, and even toys. He wagged his tail.

Then he saw it . . .

Another dog in the store. The small canine was in the arms of a woman with a lot of wrinkles on her face, and when Ollie looked his way, he puckered up his little face and snarled. It reminded Ollie of the mean dog in Pennsylvania even though he was small.

Ollie leapt from the shopping cart he'd been riding in, forgetting he was still sore. After a yelp from the pain, he ran to the woman, jumped up, and nipped at her dress. He didn't want to hurt her, but he thought he might nip at the tiny dog in her arms for giving him such a vicious look.

"Ollie! *Nee!*" Ada rushed to the woman, but Jeremiah darted past her and scooped

Ollie into his arms. Then it all happened so fast!

Ollie didn't mean to bite Jeremiah, but he picked him up the wrong way again. *Won't he ever learn?* Ada was talking with the woman and her vicious little dog. Jeremiah was bleeding.

And worst of all . . . Ada scowled at Ollie, which caused his heart to hurt.

I'm sorry I was bad.

CHAPTER 7

Later, they were back at Nellie and John's house, following a quiet ride, Ada cleaned and bandaged Jeremiah's wound where Ollie had bitten him. Ollie wished they knew how sorry he was. Maybe that's why he wasn't getting very much attention from anyone. He'd curled up in what used to be his favorite recliner, but this was a confusing time for him. *Is this home, or is Ada's house supposed to be my home?*

Either way, Ada was on the couch with Jeremiah, and they kept talking and talking and even moved closer to each other — almost like Ollie wasn't even there. Jeremiah smiled a lot. Ada batted her eyes at him.

What's happening?

Ollie jumped from the chair, then trotted his way across the living room, eyeing Jeremiah along the way. He raised his chin, did his best to squint his eyes at the man, then he eased into Ada's lap. He was mindful of his tummy, which was sorer after he had bolted from the shopping cart earlier.

Jeremiah scratched him behind his ears, and he had to admit that felt good. "He is a cutie," he said, causing Ollie to rethink his opinion about Jeremiah. He'd heard Nellie say that jealousy is a sin.

He did feel badly for biting Jeremiah and that he'd upset Ada. Maybe he could learn to like Jeremiah as much as he did Ada. That's how it had happened with Nellie and John. He'd adored Nellie from the beginning, but it took Ollie a while to warm up to John.

Nellie and John. Gone.

He nuzzled closer to Ada and tried to push their memory aside. He dozed off in his new owner's lap, but he awoke suddenly when she stood and carried him into the kitchen. Ollie could hear Jeremiah on the phone in the other room. Ada carefully set him on the floor in front of his food and water bowls.

But I'm not hungry or thirsty.

He gazed up at her, wondering why she'd abruptly stood and carried him to the kitchen. When she squatted down, a tear ran down her cheek while her lip trembled. Instinctively, Ollie licked her tear away. Was she crying because Ollie had misbehaved today in the store? He thought they were past that.

Jeremiah walked into the kitchen, then when Ada stood, he hugged her. Ollie wasn't sure how to feel. Part of him wanted to step in between Jeremiah and Ada but he decided against it since when Jeremiah hugged Ada, Ollie sensed that it made her feel better. She melted into his embrace.

"I shouldn't have gotten so attached to Ollie because I knew he might belong to someone else or that Nellie and John's next of kin might want him. But I know having him checked for a chip was the right thing to do." Ada leaned into Jeremiah's arms.

Someone else? What?

Then Ada and Jeremiah began to kiss and hug a lot, for a while. It reminded Ollie of Nellie and John when they were a family. Maybe this was Ollie's new family, both Ada and Jeremiah.

But where will we all live? Here? At Ada's house? And why did she mention me belonging to someone else?

Ollie was caring less and less about where they lived if he was with Ada. And Ada seemed to enjoy having Jeremiah around, so Ollie would learn to love him, too, just like he'd done with John.

■ ■ ■

Over the next couple of weeks, Ollie, Ada, and Jeremiah had settled into a routine. Ollie didn't completely understand it, but he liked it. He and Ada spent their days with Jeremiah. Sometimes they went shopping. Ollie tried to ignore other dogs so as not to upset anyone. It seemed best that way even though the hair on his back rose if another canine sniffed the air or perked his ears. Ada and Jeremiah also cleaned the property where Jeremiah was staying. The whole space took on a freshness and new life, and although it was starting to feel like Jeremiah and Ada's house, there was still one exception.

Every night before it got dark, Ada would give Jeremiah a long, affectionate hug before taking Ollie back to her house, where just Ollie and Ada would sleep. It was like having two homes, and that was okay with Ollie. Until one day everything changed, veered from the pattern he had become used to . . . and enjoyed.

Ada took Ollie off her lap and took him to his recliner, then swiped at her eyes. "It's going to be dark soon," she said to Jeremiah over her shoulder, sniffling.

Ollie wasn't sure why Ada was unhappy, but he was ready to go to his other home if something was upsetting her here.

Ada leaned down, kissed Ollie on his forehead, and through tears, she said, "I will miss you, Ollie, but you will have a new home with people who will *lieb* you the way I have . . . and the way Nellie and John did."

What? What? What? Ollie didn't always understand everything his humans said, but he perceived this conversation to be some sort of goodbye, which caused his chest to tighten as he began to pant, an effort to calm himself, which wasn't working.

After Ada stood, Jeremiah held her cheeks between his hands and kissed her. Ollie was getting used to this affectionate behavior, but he wasn't used to seeing Ada cry any more.

"I have to go." Ada eased out of Jeremiah's embrace and glanced out the window. "It will be dark soon," she said again.

Right, dark. We must go to our other home.

Ollie jumped from the recliner, stood wagging his tail, and waited to follow Ada to the door after she stopped hugging and kissing Jeremiah.

But following another long kiss at the door, Ada rushed outside, closing the door behind her and leaving Ollie alone with

Jeremiah. Ollie's heart flipped in his chest, and not in a good way. He jumped up on the couch and propped his front paws on the back of the cushion to get a better view out the window, unable to stop himself from whimpering. *Ada, come back! Don't leave me!* He whimpered louder.

"I know, fella. *Mei* heart is breaking too." Jeremiah lifted Ollie into his arms, not the correct way, but better. Ollie wanted to know why he wasn't going with Ada like he did every night. "But *mei mamm,* Lavina, is really looking forward to you living with her," Jeremiah said. "It will be like a part of Nellie and John are still with her." Jeremiah paused, sighing. "And we've finished all the work and cleaning on the *haus* so we can sell it."

Ollie liked when humans addressed him as if he were one of them, but this news left an uncertain outcome.

Jeremiah carried Ollie to his bed and patted the extra pillow. "Get comfy while I take a shower."

Get comfy? Where is Ada?

Ollie waited until Jeremiah was out of sight before he leapt from the bed and trotted back to the living room. He resumed his position on the couch, his front paws pressing against the back cushion as he looked out into a star-filled night, unable to stop whimpering. Ada was gone.

He heard Jeremiah talking to someone on the phone a while later and didn't understand what was happening. But when Jeremiah said, "*Gut nacht, Mamm.* Ollie and I will see you tomorrow evening," Ollie held his breath and waited for more.

But Jeremiah placed the phone on the coffee table, then he picked up Ollie and carried him back to the bedroom. Ollie wanted to run back to the couch to keep watching for Ada to return, but when Jeremiah swiped at his eyes, Ollie's heart warmed toward the man.

He wasn't sure what was happening, but it seemed to Ollie that Jeremiah might be almost as sad as Ollie was, so he decided to sleep in his bed . . . just this one night . . . until he could get home to Ada.

The next morning, Ollie wasn't hungry and stood staring at his bowls filled with food and water.

"What's the matter, fella?" Jeremiah asked from where he was sitting at the kitchen table eating breakfast. "Aren't you hungry?"

No. I'm not. I'm confused and unhappy. Where's Ada?

Jeremiah stood, still chewing, and took

two pieces of bacon, crumbled it up, and added it to Ollie's food bowl.

Sad as he was, bacon was an addiction, and he devoured all his food.

The next thing he knew, he was in one of Ada's portable kennels and in the backseat of a car driven by a man he didn't know. Jeremiah sat up front with the stranger, making Ollie feel even worse than he already did. As much as he wanted to stay awake, his eyes were as heavy as his heart. Where was Jeremiah taking him?

Ollie dozed on and off, feeling full as a tick from eating too much. But during his waking moments, his eyes searched for Ada — within the car and outside as they drove. The landscape was becoming unfamiliar, not like where Ada and Jeremiah lived. They left behind fields with farmhouses and buggies traveling on the roads to a busy highway with lots of cars and big trucks. Where was Jeremiah taking him? When would they return? His heart ached, but he kept unwillingly drifting back to sleep. A full belly had that effect.

He had no idea how long they had been in the van when they finally came to a stop and the driver turned off the engine. Nightfall had set in, and Ollie strained his neck from his spot in the kennel. He could see outside where big lamps lit the yard around him.

Where am I?

Jeremiah unloaded his suitcases and some boxes and set them on the ground.

What about me? Ollie's breathing became ragged, and he was starting to panic. He didn't know the man driving the car. Was Jeremiah going to leave him too? Ollie felt tears welling in the corners of his eyes, the ones humans didn't see, and he began to tremble.

Then familiar strong hands unhooked the latch on the kennel, and Jeremiah carefully lifted him out, the correct way this time. Ollie couldn't stop panting, but he did give Jeremiah a quick lick on the face, so he'd know he was grateful not to be forgotten and left in the vehicle. All this change was too much to handle.

Jeremiah thanked the man for transporting them, as the man helped by carrying the luggage and boxes to the front porch. Jeremiah followed toward the house with Ollie still in his arms.

They were on their way up the porch steps when Ollie realized where he was.

Oh no.

CHAPTER 8

Upon arrival, Ollie recognized where he was, and this was Buster's territory. The Blue Heeler made it clear to Ollie that he was an intruder in his home, though Ollie tried to assure him that he had no say in the matter. Ollie simply wanted to get along, and even offered to share his ball with Buster. One morning, Ollie reluctantly offered up some bacon Lavina had given him with breakfast. Buster snatched the bacon from Ollie's bowl, but it didn't change things between them. Buster was the boss in this household, and he continued to snarl, growl, and bare his teeth to let him know he was the alpha. Ollie tried to find solace in the woman named Lavina, who was nice to Ollie over the next few weeks. He remembered being in this house with Nellie and John on vacation before his life was turned upside down.

Jeremiah didn't live in the house, and he

only stopped by occasionally, giving him a familiar scratch behind the ears, though he often came bearing treats. Perhaps Jeremiah had forgotten about Ada, but Ollie couldn't shrug off the memory of the woman who saved his life. He missed sleeping on her bed, how she smelled like lavender, and the aroma of something freshly baked lingering in the air. Sometimes, it smelled like his peanut butter treats. That was his home. Second to that had been Nellie and John's house where Jeremiah, Ada, and Ollie had spent so much time together.

Where he lived now did not feel like home. Ollie spent most of his time avoiding Buster.

Ollie had brief moments of joy when Lavina cuddled him in her lap, but mostly he stayed on edge, worried if Buster was lurking nearby. Even though the other canine was constantly being reprimanded for his behavior toward Ollie, things were not getting any better. He missed Ada, and he didn't understand how she could just let him leave. Ollie had seen the sadness in her eyes, witnessed her tears. He would never understand humans. Didn't she realize that Ollie would have done anything for her? Didn't she know how much he loved her?

Today, Buster was out in the barn with

Elijah Huyard, the man of the house, while Ollie snuggled up on a blanket on the couch. He tried to sleep. It was the only time he didn't think about his past lives. He'd heard that cats had nine lives, so maybe dogs did too. But Ollie wasn't enjoying this particular life.

Jeremiah walked into the room, and Ollie's ears perked up. Over the weeks since he'd been here, Jeremiah had continued to bring him treats whenever he stopped by to visit his parents, Lavina and Elijah, and he always took time to pet Ollie. They weren't as tasty as the treats Ada had made for him, but Ollie appreciated the gestures.

Ollie had been fortunate to have so many people love him, but he still held a fondness for Nellie and John, even though he knew from Lavina's whispered prayers late at night that they weren't coming back into his life. They were with God. But surely God wouldn't have taken away Ada too. Ollie wished Jeremiah would just take him back to Ada's house so he could give her some comfort as well.

As Jeremiah and his mother chatted, Ollie yawned.

"*Mamm,* even if that were the case, I have a *haus* and a job here. Ada has a *haus* and a great community where she lives," Jeremiah said to his mother. Ollie was suddenly wide awake when he heard Ada's name as he raised an ear to hear better. "It's just not geographically possible for us to share a life together."

Yes, it is! Ollie nodded, but no one seemed to notice.

"*Gott* has a way of turning tragedy into *gut*," Lavina said. "If sweet Ollie hadn't survived, you probably wouldn't have spent so much time with Ada. And the way you've been moping around since you returned home tells me that you miss her."

Ollie rarely heard them talk about Ada, and even though he didn't always understand the conversations going on around him, he tried to fine tune what they were saying. Lavina's eyes were moist. Ollie was tempted to nuzzle her, to smother her with kisses, and let her know he was here for her even if he didn't want to be. But he didn't want to interrupt their conversation since they were talking about his beloved Ada.

"All things are possible when you draw on the strength of Christ. And when *Gott* opens a door, it's always a path that *He* has chosen for you." Lavina swiped at her eyes. "*Sohn* . . . life is short." Lavina paused, sniffling. "I don't want you to waste a minute of yours."

Jeremiah sighed. "*Mamm,* I *lieb* you, and I can see where you are going with this, but it's an impossible situation."

Lavina blinked her eyes a few times, but then she smiled. "Nothing is impossible."

Jeremiah shook his head and left the room. Lavina stood for a moment with her head slumped before she also exited the den. And Ollie was left alone with his thoughts, unsure of his future, but keeping one eye open, the way he always did, in case Buster found his way into the room.

It was a few weeks later when Jeremiah packed Ollie into the kennel that he'd brought him in to Lavina's house and loaded Ollie into a van like the one he'd arrived in. Jeremiah had also packed a lot of boxes in the vehicle as if this wasn't going to be a quick trip to the market or to visit friends.

Lavina had coddled him, kissed him on his snout, and tearfully told him she would miss him. While there was a sense of relief that he might finally be away from Buster, he liked Lavina. "You've brought me so much comfort, Ollie. A connection to Nellie and John. But someone else needs you more than I do."

Who? What does that mean? Where are you

taking me now? How many homes will I have before I'm part of a real family? Ollie felt like the baggage piled all around, just something else to be hauled off. He covered his face with his paws inside the kennel as the man driving started the motor on the car. Ollie felt spent, the same way he was when he'd left Ada behind. He could only assume that this would be another long ride.

The driver stopped twice en route to wherever they were headed so that Jeremiah could let Ollie out to do his business, but he felt sluggish. At least there was a soft, warm blanket inside the kennel that he could use to help him sleep during this long ride.

When they finally arrived at their destination, Ollie felt alert for the first time because he couldn't believe what he was seeing. They were back at Nellie and John's house. He'd given up hope that he would ever see his first family, but would Ada be inside? His heart leapt at the thought.

After Jeremiah took him from the kennel and set him on the ground, Ollie took off across the yard and trotted up the porch steps, wagging his tail, barking with all the energy he possessed.

"You recognize this place, Ollie?" Jeremiah asked as he balanced a box on one hip while he unlocked the door.

Ollie brushed past Jeremiah, crossed over the threshold, then ran from room to room downstairs before giving the upstairs equal attention. He wanted to shout Ada's name, but instead he barked so she would know he was home.

After a complete inspection, he jumped up on the familiar recliner, covered his snout with his paws, and cried on the inside. *Ada isn't here.* And, as happy as he was to be back in his original house, it didn't feel like a home without Ada. Ollie decided he should be grateful to Jeremiah for bringing him back here, but was this only a temporary trip? Would he be ripped away from the familiarity he craved?

Later in the afternoon, a big truck pulled into the driveway. It was so large that it barely fit in the space. When men started moving furniture into the house, Ollie's hope skyrocketed. This appeared to be a permanent move. Surely Ada would be here soon too.

When Jeremiah spooned food into one bowl and filled the second one with water, Ollie finally had an appetite and scarfed down what he'd been offered, lapping up water when he was done. He cringed at the name Hank still on his bowls, but he could live with that if Ada would just come home.

It was a busy day with furniture being moved out and other household items being moved in. Ollie stayed in his recliner, fearful the people moving furniture would try to take his chair. He spread out his paws against the cushion to claim it every time someone came close. He was prepared to defend his spot, although his growling days were behind him. He'd leave that business to Buster.

Hours went by and no Ada. Jeremiah fed Ollie again, although he wasn't as hungry this evening. He cared for Jeremiah, and he was happy to be back in Nellie and John's house, but his person was missing.

"I bet you're happy to be back here and away from Buster," Jeremiah said to Ollie as he carried him to the bedroom and placed him on the bed.

Yes, I am. But Ollie had only spent a few nights at the foot of this bed, and then, he'd been taken far away to a house where he'd never fully belonged — with a Blue Heeler who didn't want him as a playmate. Would he be whisked away tomorrow morning? Again? He wasn't sure he would survive another move, especially if he was being shipped to strangers. Why didn't anyone permanently want him?

Ollie had watched his humans press their palms together, then talk to someone called God, who seemed to be very important. They didn't always talk out loud, but when they did, they thanked God for things like the food on the table and special things that happened that day. They also asked Him for things, such as blessings for their harvest, good health for their family, and they always promised that they would try to live their lives based on goodness and God's will.

As nightfall came, Ollie had lost hope that Ada would be joining them. She'd had plenty of time to visit Ollie, and it was a short drive by buggy to her house. Ollie's heart sunk even more with the realization that Ada must not love him as much as he loved her.

After Jeremiah began to snore, unaware that Ollie was crying on the inside, he decided to try something new. He closed his eyes and spoke to God in his mind, the way he'd heard others speak aloud.

Dear Gott, *thank you for bringing me back to Nellie and John's house. Please don't let Jeremiah send me away tomorrow. I will live here without Ada if that is Your will. But can I ask You to please bring her back to me?*

He didn't know if his request would be honored, but a warm feeling came over him, a suggestion of sorts that everything might be all right.

Ollie awoke the next morning to the sound of voices, but he wasn't motivated to jump off the bed. He'd tossed and turned all night, worrying and curious about this new housing situation, despite that warm feeling that had settled over him. But his chest tightened when he finally yawned and realized the bedroom door was closed. Where was Jeremiah? Why was Ollie confined to the bedroom? Panic rose up through his chest, and his temptation to bark was overwhelming, but instead he hopped from the bed and tiptoed on his paws to the door to listen to the voices.

He recognized Jeremiah talking. "I *lieb* you, Ada. I've *liebed* you from the first moment I saw you." Ollie's tail wagged so hard that he thought it might snap in two, but he needed to hear the rest before he let himself get too excited. Then their voices got muffled. *What's happening?*

He barked as loud as he could so Ada would hear him. Moments later, the door flung open, and Jeremiah was smiling broadly. "She's here, Ollie."

He ran with all his might, slipping and sliding on the wood floors, but when he saw

Ada kneeling down with her arms wide open, Ollie thought his heart might explode as he jumped into her arms. His Ada began to cry. "*Ach, mei* sweet boy. I've missed you!" Ollie covered her in wet kisses. *I've missed you too!*

After Ada had officially welcomed him back, she lifted him into her arms and turned to Jeremiah. "But what about your *mamm*? I thought Ollie brought her comfort?"

"*Mamm liebed* Ollie, but *mei daed's* dog, Buster, wasn't having any part of Ollie," Jeremiah said.

No kidding! Ollie showered Ada with more kisses.

"And *Mamm* knew how hard it was for you to say goodbye to Ollie, so she wanted you to have him." Jeremiah smiled as he reached over and scratched Ollie behind his ears. "*Mamm* knew that me living in Nellie and John's *haus* was like having a part of them still with us. But that wasn't *mei* main reason for buying this *haus*, and I think you know that." He leaned around Ollie and kissed Ada for a long time. Ollie didn't think he would have shared Ada with anyone other than Jeremiah. He had missed her too.

I'm home.

EPILOGUE

For six months, things went back to normal. Ollie stayed with Ada during the evenings, and when Jeremiah wasn't working, they spent time with him during the day.

Ollie had learned to fetch his tennis balls even better. He had four of them now. His food and water bowls now said Ollie instead of Hank. And there was always an abundance of Ada's peanut butter treats. Sometimes, he even got bacon with his breakfast.

Ada worked sometimes too. She took care of other animals. At first Ollie wasn't happy that other animals were in the house, but he didn't want to act like Buster. Instead, he learned to adjust when he began to understand that Ada helped these other furry critters the same way that she had helped him. But when they were well, they went back to their own homes with their owners. A few really sick animals stayed overnight, but mostly Ollie stayed by Ada's side.

Then, one day, the most wonderful thing happened. Jeremiah and Ada got married, and they all three lived at Jeremiah's house. They renovated Ada's smaller house into a veterinarian's office and shelter for homeless animals. Ada still cared for animals when she could, but she hired someone with an animal science degree as an assistant technician, so she'd have more time to be a wife.

Ollie had settled into a life of options. Sometimes, he went to work with Ada when she chose to go. Other days, he stayed with Jeremiah out in the workshop.

He'd heard Ada, Jeremiah, and others say that God created miracles out of tragedy. Ollie was older and understood a little more about that now. He still thought about Nellie and John, but there was comfort living in their home.

Ollie recalled his prayer to God, knowing He must have heard Him because He answered by giving Ollie his forever home. Ollie had heard Ada tell Jeremiah that while they could never understand the things God does in our lives, He is always working for our good. Ollie agreed and prayed that he would always be with Ada and Jeremiah, that he would never take their love for granted.

OLLIE'S PEANUT BUTTER TREATS

Ingredients

1 cup toasted wheat germ
2 cups flour (whole wheat)
1/2 tsp. ground cinnamon
3/4 cup water
1/4 cup peanut butter (creamy)
1 large egg
2 T. Canola oil

Instructions

Preheat the oven to 350 degrees. Combine wheat germ, flour, and cinnamon, then stir in remaining ingredients. Roll dough out on a floured surface to 1/4" thickness. Cut cookies using a 3" bone-shaped cookie cutter.

Place cookies two inches apart on an ungreased baking sheet. Bake 30-35 minutes until bottoms are lightly browned. Cool thoroughly on a wire rack.

ACKNOWLEDGMENTS

Always a huge Thank You to God for continuing to bless me with stories to tell.

To my husband, Patrick, thanks for loving me AND our fur babies!

Audrey Wick and Janet Murphy, you're both fabulous! Thank you for revising and proofing my manuscripts. They always shine brighter because of your efforts. I'm so grateful and appreciate you both very much.

And, to my readers . . . without you, I wouldn't be able to continue doing what I love while hopefully entertaining you and glorifying God. A BIG THANK YOU!

ABOUT THE AUTHOR

Bestselling and award-winning author **Beth Wiseman** has sold over 3 million books. She is the recipient of the coveted Holt Medallion, a two-time Carol Award winner, and has won the Inspirational Reader's Choice Award three times. Her books have been on various bestseller lists, including CBD, CBA, ECPA, and *Publishers Weekly*. Beth and her husband are empty nesters enjoying country life in south central Texas.

The employees of Thorndike Press hope you have enjoyed this Large Print book. All our Thorndike Large Print titles are designed for easy reading, and all our books are made to last. Other Thorndike Press Large Print books are available at your library, through selected bookstores, or directly from us.

For information about titles, please call:
 (800) 223-1244

or visit our website at:
 gale.com/thorndike

